A
FOR BEN

<u>To</u>

Neil,

God bless, thanks for the football.

Love from
Elizabeth + Glenda.
xx.

FAMILY

A FAMILY FOR BEN

Gail Vinall

Scripture Union
130 City Road, London EC1V 2NJ.

By the same author:
The Project – Tiger Book
Stand out in a Crowd – Swift Book
Mirror Image – Swift Book

© Gail Vinall 1990
First published 1990

ISBN 0 86201 608 8

Phototypeset by Input Typesetting Ltd, London
Printed and bound in Great Britain by Cox and Wyman
Ltd, Reading

Chapter One

'I don't want to go!'

'You're *going*, young man, whether you like it or not.'

'Can't make me,' Ben muttered under his breath but Lillie wasn't taking any notice of him. She knew Ben well enough not to try arguing with the small but very stubborn boy. Ben scowled at the plate of spaghetti hoops he'd been eating and pushed them aside. He wasn't hungry any more.

'Where are you going?'

'Upstairs!' Ben grunted rudely. He slammed the kitchen door as he left but almost at once wished he hadn't. Lillie was all right really; in fact he quite liked her. She'd been one of the houseparents at Haven Children's Home ever since Ben had arrived when he was six years old. Now he was nine and there had been a lot of changes. Most of the fifteen kids in his home were new. The really little ones never stayed long because families wanted to adopt them, or they went to foster homes. Sometimes kids even went back to their own mums and dads. That wouldn't happen for him though. His mum had died when he was a baby, so he didn't even remember her. Ben remembered his dad but didn't bother thinking about him. The last time Ben had seen him was just before the policeman had come to drive him to Haven Children's Home. Three whole years and he hadn't ever sent a postcard, let alone come to visit. Still, who cared? Ben thought. He reached under his bunk bed and slid out a tatty carrier bag full of leaflets and magazines. They were all about cars and engines. Ben smiled and started sorting through them.

About an hour later the door opened and a tall skinny lad with masses of freckles all over his face walked in. Ben glanced up. It was Steve. He was nearly seventeen, the oldest boy in the home.

'Here, Titch, got something for you!' Steve said, reaching into his canvas bag.

A rolled-up magazine came flying across the room and landed with a thud on the floor. Ben's eyes sparkled as he flattened the creases out. It was the new BMW brochure with all the price lists.

'Cor, fantastic, Steve. Thanks.'

'Doesn't take much to keep you happy, mate!' Steve laughed. He started to take off his trainers and then remembered something. 'Oh yeah, Lillie says you've to go and see Paul.'

Paul was the house-father. Ben's smile immediately faded and he sat hugging his knees moodily.

'What's up? You in trouble?' Steve asked.

Ben shook his head. He didn't dare to speak in case the words came out all wobbly. He didn't want to go to any new foster home. Steve shrugged and sprawled across his bed.

'You'd better hop it, kid, and find out what's up.'

Ben lovingly scooped his collection of car magazines up and pushed them back under the bed. There wasn't room for any more in his locker and anyway, you had to be careful the little kids didn't get hold of them.

Pip and Sarah were playing with dolls on the stairs so Ben had to walk down on tiptoe to avoid them. Wherever you went there were bodies. It was impossible to find a private space or get any peace. As Ben passed the mirror in the hall he caught sight of himself. As usual his brown hair was falling in his eyes. Lillie said he looked like an Old English sheepdog. His face was just ordinary – the sort you'd never remember. He practised curling his top lip and was quite pleased. He could look pretty hard when he tried.

Paul was at his desk in the lounge. There was an open file in front of him, and he had a letter in one hand.

'Come and sit down, Ben.'

Ben slouched in a tatty armchair and avoided looking at Paul.

'Lillie tells me you weren't very pleased at the good news.'

'It isn't good, not for *me!*' Ben said defiantly.

'Did Lillie tell you about Mr and Mrs Thomas?'

'No, and I don't want to know 'cos I'm not going.'

'Look, Ben, I'm flattered to think that you like us all so much that you don't want to leave us . . .'

'It's not that,' Ben interrupted.

'Oh I *see!*' Paul laughed.

'If you *make* me go I'll just be so bad that they'll send me back, like I was before!' Ben threatened.

Paul's face became serious, and he leaned forward in his chair.

'Now look, Ben, you behaved in a very silly way with the Smiths. They were nice people . . .'

'They weren't! They had two daft girls who wanted me to play Sindy House. I hated them all and I'm going to hate this lot . . . and I'm going to smash their dolls' house up so they can't wait to get rid of me!' Ben was red in the face and his hands were in tight fists as he finished shouting.

'Ben, listen to me a minute. I know you didn't enjoy

9

your last foster home but please try and give this one a chance. You need a home and a family of your own.'

'I don't need anyone!' Ben insisted. 'And if you make me go I'll hate every minute . . . and I'm not even going to speak to any stupid girls.'

'Don't be silly, Ben. For a start, there aren't any girls. Mr and Mrs Thomas have one son called Peter, who's ten. You could be great friends if you make an effort. They know lots about you and they're dying to meet you.'

'I'm not going!'

Ben knew he was acting like a little kid but he didn't care. How else could he show Paul that he just wasn't interested in having any more people coming to look him over?

'We do know what's best for you, Ben. They're coming on Saturday to pick you up – all the way from Cadmouth.'

'But that's the first day of the holidays!' Ben wailed.

'Exactly! This is going to be like your first real holiday. Six weeks by the sea. You'll love it. It's a trial, that's all. If you like them, and they like you, we'll make it permanent. If not, you'll be back for the first day of term in September. Now how does that sound?'

It sounded awful, but there was no point arguing with adults. They never listened or cared what you said.

'I won't like it,' he muttered, as he trudged out of the room.

Upstairs, he went back to his magazines but even that wasn't enough to cheer him up. Only four days and then he'd be packed off. He'd been looking forward to the summer holidays, but now he wished the school term would never end.

Ben behaved so badly over the next four days that Lillie was counting the hours until the Thomas family arrived.

'You're turning into a very aggressive boy, Ben Daw-kins!' she told him after having to break up yet another fight in the lounge.

'Well, I wanted to watch that cartoon and they turned the channel over . . .'

'You don't hit out just because you can't get your own way. Now you can come and help me in the kitchen.'

'But . . .'

Ben couldn't get the words out because Lillie had hold of his collar and he had to concentrate on breathing and dodging furniture as he was hauled away. He sat at the kitchen table glaring at the pile of broad beans in front of him, while Lillie stirred a saucepan on the cooker.

'I don't know what's got into you these days,' she grumbled.

Ben curled his lip at her back and picked up a bean. He dug his nails into the skin and slid them down. Green juice squirted out of the skin and then he saw five beans nestled in the fluffy white lining. He liked to think about how he was the first person in the whole world to see those beans. After a while he had an idea for a bean machine. He laid three open bean skins end to end across the rims of two mugs. The end hung over the bowl where he already had a pile of shelled beans. Now he had a chute to transport the beans from where he was shelling them at one side of the table to the bowl at the other. It worked fairly well for a while but then there was a traffic jam and the chute collapsed, tipping the beans into one of the mugs, which still had tea dregs at the bottom.

'I don't believe it! Can't you even do a simple job without causing chaos!'

'But it's my bean machine.'

'I'll give you bean machine!' Lillie cried, sweeping the mugs and the skins off the table. 'Perhaps the Thomases will be able to teach you some proper manners.'

Ben frowned. Lillie had managed to say the one thing that was sure to make him miserable.

'A nice Christian family – that's just what you need,' Lillie continued.

'What?' Ben said, suddenly taking notice.

'The Thomases – your new family. Well, didn't Paul tell you all about them? This is their first go at fostering, you know. And they're a lovely Christian family.

'Yuk!'

'What's the matter now?' Lillie said.

'I don't want to go to any lovely Christian family. They'll be dead boring and wet . . . and they'll be saying prayers all over the place. They might even make me go to church!'

The look of horror on Ben's face was so funny that Lillie started to laugh.

'Oh, Ben,' she said, 'you are a funny boy!'

'I don't think it's very funny!' Ben shouted, his brown eyes flashing with indignation.

Lillie gulped to try and swallow another fit of giggles. 'Look, love, I don't know where you've got your ideas about Christians from but why not wait and see, before you make your mind up? I think you're going to be very surprised when you meet the Thomases.'

Lillie was right about *that,* at least. Ben had formed a very different picture of Peter from the real boy who arrived at two o'clock on Saturday afternoon with his parents. From the upstairs window Ben saw the car pull up in the drive. He watched a tall, dark-haired man in a tweed jacket get out of the driver's side. The car was a blue Escort Ghia. He wouldn't mind a go in that anyway. Now the woman was getting out. She had long, fair hair tied back, and she was smoothing down her skirt and talking a lot. The sound of her high voice floated up to Ben. Was their son with them? Ben craned his neck to catch a glimpse but couldn't tell if anyone had got out of the back seat.

He turned back to his bed and finished stuffing the last of his clothes into a tatty old duffle bag. There wasn't any room for his magazines or his jam jar full of nuts and bolts. He'd have to carry them.

'Do you *have* to take all that junk with you?' Lillie had asked, when she'd been helping him pack earlier on. Ben had kicked up such a fuss, though, that she had found him a jar with a proper screw top lid to put them in.

Now he could hear his name being called. Ben looked round the familiar bedroom with a lump in his throat. It wasn't as if it was his own room – in fact he'd always hated having to share it with so many others – but it felt sort of cosy now that he had to leave it.

'Bye, Steve,' he called, dragging the duffle bag across the floor.

'Oh yeah, see you, kid,' Steve called but without raising his eyes from a newspaper. 'You enjoy yourself.'

'I shan't!' Ben said hotly, 'And I'm going to be back here in September.'

'Oh yeah? Well, whatever you say, Titch.'

Even Steve didn't believe him, but they'd see. They could make him go but they couldn't make him stay. And even if the Thomases were saints they'd soon get tired of *him*! In this frame of mind, Ben banged his bag viciously down the stairs and left it in the hall where everyone would trip over it. He put his other possessions carefully on the table and then slouched towards the lounge where he could hear Paul talking. His hands were stuffed deep in his pockets and he kicked the lounge door open with his foot, making Mrs Thomas jump. Paul smiled knowingly and didn't react.

'Ah, right on cue. This is Ben, everyone.'

Ben had decided to keep his mouth tightly shut but as the boy, who had to be Peter, stood up he couldn't help gawping. Peter was a giant, compared to him anyway. He must be easily a foot taller and he looked very strong as well. Like his mother, he was blonde but his hair was carefully spiked and razor cut at the back in the latest style. He wore light blue denim jeans and jacket, both of which looked brand new. He was sizing Ben up too, from the look on his face and Ben knew just what he'd be seeing. The tatty trainers splitting at one toe; jeans not quite long enough and patched on both knees; shirt, jumper and anorak all different colours, none of them matching. He felt smaller than ever and horribly inferior. He even forgot to curl his lip at the boy as he'd been intending to. What was the point? This giant could flatten him with one hand tied behind his back.

Mr Thomas nudged his son, who was staring back at Ben.

'Hello, Ben, I'm Peter. Nice to meet you.'

Ben grunted in reply. He didn't have any well rehearsed lines for Peter or the adults who were trying not to look nervous.

'Are you all packed, Ben?' Paul asked, to break the uncomfortable silence.

Ben nodded, head down.

'Well, that's about it, then. You've a long drive ahead of you and if you've finished your tea, I'll gather the farewell party.'

The two adults put down their cups and started

making bright comments about how nice the home was and what a lovely cake Lillie had made.

Ben felt his stomach doing somersaults as they made for the front door. Lillie half-crushed him in a great bear hug, and Ben had to wipe off several wet kisses, blushing furiously as he did so.

'Here I'll help you,' Peter said as Ben dragged his bag across the floor. Peter flung the duffle bag over his shoulder as if it was as light as a feather.

'Can I take something?' Mr Thomas asked.

'No,' Ben replied rather sharply as he hugged the carrier bag of magazines and the jar to his chest.

'Oh, you won't get your hands on those!' Lillie laughed. 'His pride and joy they are, though what you'll do with all that junk I don't know.'

Ben glared at Lillie to make her be quiet. She could be so embarrassing.

'Don't worry, I'm used to worse than that,' Mrs Thomas smiled.

'There's plenty of cupboard space in your room at home, Ben,' she added.

Ben ignored her. It wasn't *his* room or *his* home, and it would never be.

As they left Havens, Ben sat bolt upright in the back of the car, determined not to look back at Lillie and the kids who'd gathered to wave goodbye. He wasn't going to show anyone that he cared, especially not Peter.

'I hope you'll like our house, Ben,' Mrs Thomas said, twisting round so that she could see him. 'It's quite ordinary but we've got a nice big garden. You can have your own bedroom or share with Peter. What do you think you'd like?'

'I don't care,' Ben muttered.

'Give the lad a chance, Pam!' Mr Thomas laughed, 'He might decide to catch the first bus back, eh lad?'

Ben looked at the man, surprised. He must be making his feelings pretty obvious. Or was it just that Mr Thomas was better at understanding how he felt about driving off with three complete strangers. He relaxed into the plush upholstery and watched the shops and houses flash by until they petered out altogether and there were just green hedges and the odd stone cottage. Ben had never been this far and he didn't have a clue which direction Cadmouth was. Lillie had explained that it was a small town on the coast, quite busy with tourists in summer. Being by the sea might be all right, so long as he wasn't expected to swim or dive in it. He couldn't swim at all, in fact there weren't many physical things that he was any good at. Ben glanced sideways at Peter, thinking how he'd probably be fantastic at everything from diving to table tennis. Peter caught Ben's eye and looked away. He wasn't sure what it was going to be like having a brother, and having to share things.

It was nearly seven o'clock by the time they arrived, Ben felt so tired that he barely noticed the street but the house seemed to have a lot of windows and the front door was wooden and had black iron bars across it, making it look like the entrance to a castle.

Mrs Thomas left the boys in the lounge while she cooked a quick supper. Peter switched the TV on and both boys watched it, rather than having to make awkward conversation. It was a relief to be called for supper.

They all sat at the kitchen table as Mrs Thomas flipped fried eggs and sausages onto pale blue plates. There was a big pile of crusty bread in the middle of the table and mugs of tea. It was just the sort of meal Ben loved and in spite of his bad mood he had to admit to feeling very hungry. Without asking, he shot a hand out to grab the tomato sauce. It was a fancy squirter and as his hand closed over it a jet of scarlet sauce flew up and landed

16

on Mr Thomas's plate.

'Crikey!' Ben said, as he watched the goo trickle over the eggs. To his amazement Mr Thomas laughed, and started on his eggs with enthusiasm.

'How kind of you to serve me first, Ben,' he added.

'Here, Ben, on the sausages!' Peter laughed, holding out his plate.

'I think that's enough!' Mrs Thomas smiled, taking the sauce container out of Ben's hand. She dolloped a neat circle on both boys' plates before helping herself.

Without intending to, Ben had managed to break the ice and the meal continued happily. Then Mrs Thomas and Peter took Ben upstairs. Ben was glad she had decided to give him his own room. He wanted somewhere where he could escape.

'Here you are, I hope this is OK,' Mrs Thomas said, swinging open wardrobe doors and indicating cupboards. She crossed to the window and swept the curtains together, then turned the duvet down and patted the pillow. Ben stood in the middle of the room looking and feeling very small. As if sensing this, Mrs Thomas came and put an arm around his shoulders.

'We're so pleased you're here,' she said.

Ben squirmed out of her reach and pretended to be looking at a picture on the wall.

'That's me in the school cup final last year,' Peter said, proudly. 'Do you play football for a team?'

'No.'

'Oh well, I guess your school didn't have one. Still, you like football don't you?'

'No, not much.'

'Oh!' Peter looked disappointed. 'What about tennis then?'

'Never tried.'

'Questions tomorrow!' Mrs Thomas said. 'Let Ben

17

have a minute to unpack.' She towed Peter out of the room and left Ben on his own.

His clothes didn't take much space. The three shirts and pairs of jeans looked ridiculous in the wardrobe. Still, who cared. He was a massive let-down for them all. Peter wanted an all-round sports wizard and his mum wanted a girl to cuddle. The trial wouldn't last more than a week at this rate.

Chapter Two

Ben couldn't remember where he was when he woke up the following morning. He had to lie still for several moments before he realised the sunlight was dancing up and down on his face through a crack in the curtains. It was strange to wake up in a room on your own where there was no noise. What day was it? Sunday. He strained his ears. Someone else was awake and up. He heard water hiss and gurgle through pipes and then voices.

'Peter, are you ready?' It was Mrs Thomas's high voice.

Ready for what, Ben wondered. They couldn't be going to the shops on a Sunday and it was a bit early for visiting.

'Church! I'll bet they're going to church!' Ben spoke out loud. 'Well, I'm not,' he added as he dived under the covers.

Moments later he heard the bedroom door open and someone tiptoed in.

'Ben?' Mrs Thomas whispered, uncertainly.

Ben willed himself to lie absolutely still. It seemed like hours before she slowly retreated, clicking the bedroom door shut. Ben's brown tousled head poked out of the covers and he grinned to himself. He'd never have fooled Lillie.

Not long afterwards the front door banged and a car engine started. Good, the danger was over. He could get up now. But was he alone? Had they all gone? Ben slid out of bed and rubbed his eyes. Not bothering to wash, he pulled on the clothes he'd dropped on a chair the night before and made his way downstairs.

The kitchen was deserted but there was a bowl and various boxes of cereals left out. Ben suddenly felt very alone and began to regret his trick on Mrs Thomas.

'Hello, sleepyhead!' It was Mr Thomas, dressed in greasy overalls.

Ben spun round, relief making him smile. 'Oh, I thought you'd all gone to church.'

'Just Peter and his mum. You weren't awake and my wife thought you'd be better off having a lie-in after yesterday. We couldn't leave you on your own so I volunteered to stay. I'll go tonight – make a change. Did Peter tell you about church last night?'

'No.' Ben blushed. It was obvious that he hadn't really been asleep, if he knew they had left for church.

Mr Thomas put the kettle on to make a fresh pot of tea. Ben noticed that his nails were black with engine oil. The smell of it clung to his clothes, reminding Ben of a garage he'd once been to with Steve. Mr Thomas poured milk into two mugs and waited for the tea to brew. He wore heavy steel-tipped boots and a spanner poked out of one pocket.

Ben shook cereal into a bowl and ate while Mr Thomas studied a car manual. His dark hair flopped into his eyes as he concentrated. It was comfortable just sitting with this man, not needing to talk. When he had drunk his tea, Mr Thomas rolled the manual up and bounced it lightly on Ben's head.

'Finish your breakfast and then you can come and watch me for a while. I'll be in the workshop.'

'OK,' Ben said.

After a huge bowl of Sugar Puffs, he wandered out of the back door and followed the noise of hammering to a rickety outhouse, tucked out of sight. The garden was huge and it backed on to fields, which made it seem even bigger. Near the house there were flower beds and a neat lawn but it gradually got wilder and much more interesting as you walked further. Ben leant against the door of the outhouse which groaned before giving way jerkily. It was dark and for a while Ben was blinded but then, out of the gloom, he saw the outline of a very old, very battered car. He let out a gasp of amazement.

'It's a Lanchester!'

Mr Thomas looked up from the bench where he was hammering at a piece of metal. 'I'm impressed – my wife calls it a heap of rust.'

'Where did you get it?' Ben asked, running his hand carefully along the dented wing.

'At an auction, last year. I'm afraid it's needed a lot more work done on it than I'd thought and time is a big problem. Still, it'll be beautiful when I've finished.'

'I love cars,' Ben breathed, almost to himself.

Mr Thomas watched him as he fingered the instrument panel lovingly. 'Well, you'd better give me a hand then. Do you know anything about engines?'

Ben nodded proudly.

'What's this, then?' Mr Thomas grinned, holding up a dirty lump of metal.

Ben squinted at it. 'Carburettor!' he announced.

'Think you could get it cleaned up – bright as a new pin?'

'Sure!'

Ben found a rag, emery paper and white spirit on the bench and started work.

Mr Thomas watched the front of Ben's shirt become

streaked with grease but said nothing. If the lad was really keen on helping, he'd get him a pair of overalls later.

Ben's nimble fingers worked away. He was totally engrossed in the task. It didn't matter that it was slow and monotonous. He liked the smell of the place and the rows of spanners, sockets, grips and screwdrivers which lined the walls. Mr Thomas's strong hands were professional and Ben felt a deep respect for their skill. The two didn't need to talk much and for the first time since leaving Havens, Ben could show he was good at something.

It wasn't until Peter came barging into the workshop, yelling that dinner was ready, that Ben realised how the hours had sped by.

'Hey, what're you doing here?' Peter said.

Cross that they'd been disturbed, Ben felt antagonism rise inside him.

'Ben's been a great help,' Mr Thomas answered, wiping his hands on a rag. 'Which is more than I can say for some people, who just come in here to mess around!'

'Aw, it's just a load of old rust!' Peter said. He was jumping around, practising boxing shots at an imaginary partner. 'Here, Dad – heard a daft joke this morning.'

'Go on then.'

'Three teddy bears in the airing cupboard. How do you know which one's in the army?'

'I don't know.'

'The one that's sitting on the tank! Get it?'

Mr Thomas chuckled. 'Yes, I get it and yes, it's daft! Come on . . .'

Father and son wandered out together. Apparently Peter had several more jokes to tell. Ben followed at a distance. He'd had a great morning but now he felt fed up, and he didn't know why. Something in his head told him it was because he was jealous of Peter. Jealous of the way he could make people laugh – jealous of his confidence and his size. Jealous most of all because he'd got a dad to muck around with. Well, I don't need anyone, Ben reminded himself as he followed them up to the house.

There was an appetising smell of roast pork in the air as they went into the house. The table was laid in the dining room and Mrs Thomas was carrying steaming dishes of vegetables through. She smiled at Ben, not commenting on his filthy clothes. He was steered to the kitchen sink by Mr Thomas who squirted washing-up liquid into his hands, and together they cleaned up.

Ben reached for his knife and fork as soon as they sat down to eat but stopped when the others all bowed their heads.

'Ben, we like to say grace before our main meal each day,' Mrs Thomas explained. She looked at Peter who said a short prayer thanking God for the food.

Ben scowled at his plate, refusing to close his eyes or say 'Amen' at the end. How daft, he thought. God hadn't gone out to the shops or cooked the food, so what were they all thanking *him* for? He'd told Lillie it was going to be prayers all over the place. Ben almost considered going on hunger strike in protest but everything smelt too good. He had to admit Mrs Thomas wasn't a bad cook.

After lunch, Mr Thomas disappeared to read a paper while the boys wiped up. At Havens there had been a rota for chores so Ben was used to doing housework.

'What shall we do this afternoon, then?' Peter said, throwing his wet tea-towel across a rail when they'd finished.

'Don't mind,' Ben replied dully. He would have liked

to do some more work on the carburettor but Peter obviously had other ideas.

'I'll show you the garden, then we'll go over the fence and muck about in the field. We could have a kick around, Oh, I forgot, you don't play football, do you?'

Ben looked up sharply. Was Peter having a go at him? It was hard to tell.

'Off you go, then. Don't hurt yourselves and be back for tea,' Mrs Thomas said.

Ben and Peter trudged through the long grass at the bottom of the garden without saying much. Peter had tried his best, but all his questions got the shortest possible answer or even no answer. He had a feeling Ben wasn't that keen on him.

'Hey, shall we go and explore the barn?' he finally suggested as a last resort.

'Where is it?' Ben said, curious in spite of himself.

'In the dip. You can't see it from here. Come on, I'll show you.'

Peter raced off and was over the fence in seconds. It took Ben longer to find a proper foothold and he almost lost sight of Peter by the time he was clear of it.

'Sorry, I'm a faster runner than most people,' Peter said when Ben finally caught him up. It wasn't said in a boastful way but just as a matter of fact.

'Yeah, Well, I didn't hurry,' Ben said, gasping for breath and wondering whether his lungs were really on fire.

'Here, have a sweet,' Peter said.

They walked on together, Peter keeping up a commentary on who the barn belonged to and other times when he'd explored it.

'There's just hay in it at the moment but up the top there's some old farm machinery. Ploughs and bits of harness I think.'

24

'Really?' Ben perked up a bit. 'You don't like your dad's old car, do you?' he added.

'Not much,' Peter grinned. 'He spends hours in there when Mum and I want to go out. I'm no good helping him. I get bored and start dropping things, then he has a fit! I wish Dad would join a golf club or something then I could go with him. I'd love to learn to play.'

'You like *all* sports?'

'Yeah, it's great – I'd love to have a go at loads more sports.'

'It'll be pretty boring having me around then,' Ben said, looking him in the eye.

Peter flushed. 'Hey, I didn't mean . . . Well, sport isn't everything, I guess.'

The barn loomed ahead of them, its big double doors propped open by several rotting bales of hay. Inside, a ray of sunlight picked up swirling specks of dust. It was a huge building. The floor was strewn with corn and there were tracks through it, probably rats or mice. Scurrying, scraping noises frequently broke the silence and Ben kept checking where he was standing. He shuddered at the thought of a rat crawling over his toes, especially when Peter started on about how he'd once seen a rat as big as a cat.

There were owls up in the eaves, according to Peter, but Ben couldn't see any. He wasn't quite sure what he was looking for and he didn't like to show how ignorant he was about birds by asking. They spent quite a while rooting around, turning over old boxes and looking for treasures. Peter found an old horseshoe which he put near the door to take home. Then they decided to go up the ladder which led to the upper floor. As expected, there were some interesting bits of machinery but most of it was rotting away. An old saddle had split open and mice had eaten at the stuffing. The leather girth strap was so hard and gnarled that it would have broken in two if anyone tried to bend it. The huge wheel of a trailer lay horizontally in the straw and a broken plough was upside down next to it. Peter waited while Ben spun the wheel and hauled the plough right side up to inspect it. Then there was a weird grunting noise, from quite close by.

Both boys stopped and listened. It came again.

'Rats?' Ben whispered, edging towards the ladder. His scalp seemed to have shrunk on his head.

But the grunt was this time followed by a rattling cough, which could hardly be a rat.

'There's someone up here!' Peter hissed.

'Let's go!' Ben said, his mind running on tales of escaped prisoners or desperate murderers, or even aliens from outer space.

Peter was about to follow when there was an eruption in the mound of hay near the ladder which sent them careering into each other as they tried to get away from it.

First a hand emerged from the pile then an elbow and finally a head. The boys gazed with open mouths as Bert, gentleman of the road for sixty years, woke up from his afternoon nap. He grunted several more times before giving a loud toothless yawn. Then he scratched his bristly chin with one hand and picked strands of hay out of his ear with the other.

'Huh. Can't a body get a bit of peace without being disturbed by hooligans?' Bert complained.

'You're trespassing!' Ben accused him, cross at being called a hooligan.

'So are you,' Bert replied.

'Do you live here?' Peter asked.

'At the moment, yes!'

'Well, if we told the farmer he'd kick you out,' Ben

said threateningly.

'And if I tell him you were mucking around with matches in here, you'd be for it.'

'But we haven't got any matches!' Ben protested.

'Well, he's not to know that, is he? My word against yours.'

Before this pointless argument could go any further, Peter pushed Ben towards the ladder.

'Well, we're sorry to have disturbed you and we've got to get home now.'

'Righto sonny, but listen, could you do me a favour?'

'Depends what it is,' Peter said doubtfully.

'Give us the price of a cup of tea?' Bert asked.

Peter hesitated, then felt his pockets.

'I'm sorry, I haven't got any money on me.'

'What about you, young un?' Bert asked Ben.

'No way, you old scav. I wouldn't give you anything even if I had pots of money.'

Bert scowled and muttered some threatening words under his breath.

'You'll be old yourself one day,' he grumbled.

'Yeah, but I won't be an old dosser like you, mate.'

Bert raised his scraggy head regally. 'My name is Bert Hicks and I am a traveller!' he announced.

'Yeah, a beggar,' Ben said.

'I *ask*, I don't beg.'

Peter suddenly remembered the packet of sweets in his pocket and took them out. 'Would you like these, as we haven't got any money?' he suggested.

Bert thought about it for a while and then accepted the sweets.

'Thank you, sonny. Now I'd like to have some quiet if you don't mind.'

The audience was obviously over, so the boys descended the ladder and were soon out into the sunshine again. They walked a while without speaking before Ben turned to Peter.

'What did you give him those sweets for?'

'Well, it was all I had.'

'You needn't have given him anything!'

'I wanted to,' Peter said simply. 'Anyway I thought you were a bit rude.'

'What's it to you?' Ben said, his hands forming fists.

'Nothing! There wasn't anything wrong with him, that's all, so I gave him the sweets.'

'You didn't *have* to, though,' Ben insisted.

'I know. You can give people things without having to.'

'He was a perfect stranger.'

'It doesn't matter. Last year our school collected money for children in Africa who were starving. They were strangers.'

'But he wasn't starving.'

'He wasn't very well off, though.'

'That's his fault if he chooses to be a tramp.'

'We don't know if he *did* choose and it still doesn't make any difference. There's no need to be rude to people.'

'Yeah, well you *would* say that,' Ben scoffed. 'I suppose that's what you get told at church.'

Peter tried to stay calm, but he didn't like being laughed at. 'We're told that God loves everyone, so that means we're all the same to him and we're supposed to treat everyone as we'd like them to treat us.'

Ben thought about this for a while. 'What about when people treat you rotten?' he argued.

'So?'

'Well, you've got to treat them rotten back, haven't you, else they'll know you're a wimp and they'll never stop thumping you or something.'

28

'But then you never stop fighting. I mean, no one ever wants to give up, do they?'

'Great. I like a good scrap,' Ben replied, because he couldn't think of a better argument.

Peter didn't say anything.

It wasn't really true, though. Ben didn't like fighting and he hated being picked on. He didn't really know why he'd had a go at Bert. He was fed up with Peter's soppy attitude though. God loves everyone! What a load of rubbish. If God loved everyone why had he let his dad go off and leave? God might like Peter who was a goody-goody, but not everyone.

Chapter Three

It didn't take long for Ben to convince Peter that he didn't like football. It was soon obvious that he was useless at anything which involved hitting a ball in a specific direction. The problem was that instead of just leaving it at that, and letting him go off to the workshop on his own, Peter and his mum seemed determined to help him improve. Even when he told them he didn't want to play football, or tennis, or squash! The list of games Peter and his mum enjoyed was endless.

Mrs Thomas spent an entire morning with Ben on something she called ball skills. It involved being able to catch one when it was hurled at you at a speed likely to knock your head off if you missed. The only skill Ben improved that morning was learning to duck very quickly. Then Peter suggested putting Ben in goal while he aimed all sorts of shots at him. It didn't matter whether they were long, short, high, curving or straight – Ben missed them all.

'Would you like to shoot now?' Peter had offered, as Ben picked the ball out of the net for what seemed like the millionth time.

The only sort of shooting Ben felt like doing would have involved an air rifle – aimed straight at the wretched football – but even then he would probably have missed.

Ben endured these sessions fairly calmly for several days. Even Mrs Thomas would lose patience with him soon, he thought. As far as ball skills went, she did, but the idea of turning Ben into an athlete was apparently still in her mind.

'I know what!' she announced one morning after breakfast. 'We'll take Ben swimming – that's something we can all enjoy together!'

Ben felt himself go rigid. Swimming! He couldn't swim, not even doggie paddle.

'It's freezing in the sea,' Peter moaned and Ben breathed again – but his relief was short-lived.

'That's all right – we'll drive into Cadmouth. The baths shouldn't be too crowded if we get a move on. How does that sound, Ben?'

'Well . . . I haven't got any swimming gear,' Ben said, which was true.

'No problem, I've got a spare pair of trunks!' Peter announced, as Ben had feared he would.

Mrs Thomas went upstairs to collect towels while Peter produced goggles, nose clips and trunks.

'What are those for?' Ben asked, picking up the nose clips curiously.

'Oh, they're good for diving. You can use them if you like. Look, I'll show you,' Peter demonstrated.

Diving! Things were going from bad to worse. It wasn't enough just to flounder out of your depth – now they expected him to fling himself in from a great height.

'Actually I . . .' Ben began but something stopped him. He was fed up with saying 'I'm not very good at . . .' all the time. Why couldn't he go and work on Mr Thomas's old car, which is what he'd been dying to do for the past week? If only they'd let him alone and stop trying to make him into something he couldn't be.

'I've packed an extra jumper for you, Ben,' Mrs

Thomas said. 'It can feel chilly when you get out of the water.'

An oxygen tank might be more useful, Ben thought, as he trudged out to the car.

Ben was silent all the way to Cadmouth, partly because he felt too cross at them both to talk, and partly because he was formulating a plan to survive the morning without admitting he couldn't swim. If Peter and his mum went up to the diving end, then maybe he could splash around at the shallow end and they wouldn't notice whether he was swimming or not. It was his only hope.

At the turnstiles there was quite a queue. Ben hoped wildly that Mrs Thomas would say 'Let's forget it' and they could go home, but he knew that she was the sort of person who couldn't bear to change a plan if people would be disappointed. Peter was itching to get in the water. As soon as Mrs Thomas had paid, he dashed off to the changing rooms and Ben had to jog to keep pace with him. Inside the clammy locker room Ben sniffed the chlorine in the air with a sinking sensation. He tried to put off the moment of facing the water by inventing a knot in his shoelace and taking ages to get it undone but eventually he was ready. His own spindly white legs and arms contrasted horribly with Peter's much larger, browner body. This is going to be awful, Ben thought, as he padded after Peter, wincing as they splashed through a sub-zero temperature foot bath.

The pool was vast. The roof was blue and built of huge arching steel girders and glass to make you feel as if you were on some tropical island. Palm trees in great tubs surrounded the water and people were sitting at white plastic tables under them, drinking hot chocolate or lemonade. The shallow end was a mass of bobbing heads and thrashing bodies in bright coloured swimsuits. At the far end were the diving boards, the water under them smooth and dark blue because it was so deep. There were far fewer people up there and they swam with smooth, powerful strokes like great fish.

'There's Mum, come on!' Peter said.

To Ben's relief, Mrs Thomas was only in water up to her waist. Peter flung himself in beside her and she shrieked because she wasn't all wet yet.

'Come on, Ben!' Peter yelled, as he tossed his slicked-down hair out of his eyes.

Ben sidled over to the edge of the pool and sat down, dangling his legs over. The water was surprisingly warm and it felt quite nice swishing in between his toes.

'Get in, then!' Peter yelled.

'In a minute,' Ben replied. He edged his bottom over the tiles and gasped as the tepid water hit his stomach. So far, so good. He bent his knees an inch and gradually let the water level rise up to his arm-pits.

Peter was swimming round his mum, flicking water in her face until she ducked right under the water. Her long hair floated out around her and Ben thought she looked like a mermaid he'd once seen in a picture book at school. She could swim like one too and was soon surging away towards the deep end, Peter following her. Ben retreated back to the side and kept a very firm hand on the bar as he gingerly lifted one leg off the bottom. Little kids of five or six came bobbing by him, absolutely fearless. There was even a baby in a huge rubber ring being towed along by his mother. How come everyone else had buoyant bodies when *his* would sink like a stone as soon as he let go of the bar? His teeth started to chatter and goose bumps appeared all over his arms. What a miserable way to spend a morning. Ben glanced at the huge clock on the wall and felt even worse. Only ten minutes had gone and the ticket had said you were allowed two hours in the pool.

Peter was swimming back towards him, slicing through the water like a dolphin.

'Are you coming up the other end? It's less crowded,' Peter said, showering Ben with droplets as he surfaced.

'No, I'm staying here,' Ben replied firmly.

'OK. Well , I'll give you a race then – widths. Ready? Go!'

Peter stormed off leaving a foamy wake behind him. Ben stayed where he was. Peter was waving to him from the other side but Ben pretended not to notice. Suddenly some idiot jumped in beside Ben, knocking his arm off the bar. In the tidal wave that followed, Ben's legs were swept from under him and he was down. All he could see was an underwater forest of legs, his ears were deafened by a watery roaring and blind panic gripped at his throat. As he fought to get his mouth above water for what seemed like hours, a hand suddenly cupped itself under his chin and dragged him up.

Ben surfaced with a splutter and gulped air like a demented fish. He grabbed his rescuer round the neck and clung on like a limpet, until he realised it was Mrs Thomas and she was having trouble breathing herself. She managed to lift him onto the side and then hauled herself out to sit beside him.

'Ben, are you all right? You should have said you couldn't swim! What made you jump in like that?' she cried.

Ben was about to point out that he had hardly 'jumped in' as she put it, but he felt too ashamed.

Peter swam up, and his mother turned on him.

'How *could* you, Peter! Fancy not telling me Ben can't swim – and letting me go off and leave him!'

'I didn't know he couldn't swim!' Peter exclaimed loudly.

'Oh, go on, tell the whole world, why don't you!' Ben shouted, getting to his feet.

Peter and his mum stared at each other for a moment, then Mrs Thomas took command. 'Right, hot drinks! Come on.' She grabbed Ben by the arm and sat him down at one of the plastic tables. 'Stay there!' she said and Ben obeyed.

She returned with a big red towel and her purse. A waiter set three mugs of chocolate on the table. Ben scooped off the thick froth with one finger and sucked it.

'I'm so sorry, Ben,' Mrs Thomas was saying as she rubbed his thin shoulders with the towel. He shrugged moodily. He felt such a fool. Acting like he was going to drown in less than one metre of water. Peter must be wetting himself. He glanced up but Peter didn't look as if he was laughing.

After the drink, Ben felt much better and a bit guilty about spoiling their swim. 'Look, I'll stay here while you have a swim,' he offered, but Mrs Thomas wouldn't hear of it.

'No, we'll go now. It was a silly idea and I promise we won't come swimming again.'

'He'd be all right if he learnt,' Peter said, sulkily, but Mrs Thomas shook her head.

'The attendants are paid to teach people,' Peter insisted.

'You're just being selfish because *you* don't want to go home,' his mum said quietly.

Peter stared at the other swimmers in frustration. He'd never known that having a new brother would mean giving up loads of activities he liked doing. If only Ben wasn't so useless at things. As soon as this thought came into his head, Peter felt ashamed. Ben was looking at the swimmers too. Suddenly Peter had an idea.

'Hey, why don't *I* teach you to swim?'

Ben considered. He stared at the tiny kids leaping up and down in the water and envied them. This wasn't like football and he secretly wished he *could* swim, just enough to get by.

'I wouldn't mind,' he said.

'There'd be no going off to have a swim on your own,' his mum warned.

'I know, I promise I won't leave you, Ben.'

'OK then.'

'Good one!' Peter encouraged. 'Hang on a minute.' He dashed off towards one of the attendants and returned with half a dozen arm bands.

'What do you want with all those?' Mrs Thomas asked.

'You'll see!' Peter laughed. He handed two to his mum, put two on himself and gave the final pair to Ben. 'Now Ben won't feel the odd one out,' he explained, as they all headed for the shallow end.

Mrs Thomas floated on her back a little way from the boys while Peter explained the basic actions. He was really patient and never asked Ben to do anything too scary. After half an hour of kicking his legs, holding on to the bar, Ben progressed to being towed across the pool by Peter. He knew Peter wouldn't let him go or try anything stupid, and as he relaxed he began to feel the water holding him up, rather than dragging him down. It was a good feeling. He felt tingly warm all over and he was enjoying himself. He didn't even panic when water got in his eyes.

In fact, he was just about to attempt a solo float when a couple of kids swam up beside him.

'Hey, it's the water babies,' one of them yelled.

Peter looked up but pretended to ignore them. Ben scowled. If they were on land he'd give them what for but in here he was at a distinct disadvantage.

They kept splashing near Ben, causing him to panic and rush for the side. This evidently amused them.

'Why don't you push off!' Ben yelled angrily.

'Gonna make us, kid?' they laughed, swimming just far enough so that Ben would be out of his depth if he tried to follow.

'I will, if you don't leave him alone,' Peter said quietly.

'Oh ho, it's the tough guy in his shiny yellow water wings. Tell you what, we'll give you a start, sonny, before we come after you and give you a good ducking.'

'No need,' Peter smiled, removing the arm bands. He started to swim away from Ben, with slow sure strokes. The two bullies followed, yelling threats. Peter kept just ahead of them until they reached the halfway line then trod water as if he was out of breath.

'We've got him,' one of the lads yelled and lunged forward to bounce Peter's head under water. Quickly Peter dived, swam between his attackers' legs and grabbed an ankle. Yanking the bully down, Peter released him and then surfaced.

'He nearly drowned me!' the lad was shouting but the attendant, who had only seen the first bit, was blowing on his whistle.

'If I see you trying to duck anyone again it's out!'

Peter swam away, leaving the two yobs to argue between themselves.

Ben had watched it all, with great admiration, from the shallow end.

'You showed 'em!' he grinned.

'Yeah, they got a taste of their own medicine,' Peter said. 'Right – what about your solo attempt. Feel up to it?'

Ben nodded. He was going to do it. He licked his lips nervously, took a deep breath and then pushed away from the edge. Legs and arms flailing like a windmill, he made for the opposite edge of the baths. Peter was swimming alongside, shouting encouragement in his ear and Mrs Thomas was at the opposite side willing him on. He seemed to be making no progress at all but inch by inch he bobbed through the water until Mrs Thomas was just an arm's length away and then he grabbed at the bar and she was dragging him, exhausted and panting, onto the tiles.

'Brilliant! Ace!' Peter was screaming and anyone would have thought Ben had just achieved an Olympic gold medal for the freestyle.

Ben sat on the side, his face nearly split in two with the huge grin that he couldn't stop.

'Well done!' Mrs Thomas said. 'I've never seen anyone learn so quickly.'

'Yeah well, brilliant teacher,' Peter boasted. He was surprised to find that he'd actually enjoyed helping Ben.

Ben smiled at him. He *had* been a good teacher, and swimming was OK.

'We'll have to work on your style a bit,' Peter continued.

'Another day,' Mrs Thomas said. 'Ben needs a nice hot shower now before he gets cold.'

The boys trotted off to the changing rooms, talking loudly, and Mrs Thomas watched them go, feeling happy. Her disastrous idea had turned out rather well after all, she decided.

Ben felt really tired but he got changed with a lot more enthusiasm than when they'd arrived. He was going to write to Lillie and tell her he'd learnt to swim. She'd never believe it. He'd get Mrs Thomas to write a bit on the end, just to prove it. Funny, he hadn't thought about Lillie for days. Ben suddenly realised he'd been with the Thomases a fortnight. That was a third of the time he'd be staying. Well, if the next two thirds went as quickly, it wouldn't be bad.

Ben watched Peter combing his hair in front of the mirror. In some ways he was a real poser, especially when it came to how he looked, but he'd worn those daft arm bands and spent the whole morning teaching him to swim with the little kids when he could have been diving. He'd also dealt with those yobs pretty well. Yes, he was OK in some ways. So was his mum really, if she wouldn't fuss him so much and treat him like a little kid.

On the way home the boys sat in the back discussing the next swimming lesson.

'Perhaps we'll get Dad to help Ben,' Mrs Thomas said.

'No, Ben's *my* pupil,' Peter objected. 'It's great fun getting someone to do something they've never done before.'

Fun? Ben couldn't quite believe it. Peter wasn't just teaching him because he felt he'd got to, he really enjoyed it.

'Cor, I'm starving,' Peter added.

'I've only got Polos,' Mrs Thomas said, rummaging in her pocket with one hand. 'Here!' she said, tossing a packet over her shoulder.

Without thinking, Ben put out his hand and caught them.

'Hey, did you see what Ben just did?' Peter said.

'Ball skills!' Ben laughed.

Once they got home Ben had intended disappearing upstairs to read some new car magazines Mr Thomas had bought him but instead he watched TV with Peter. It was all right being with him today and in any case, there'd be plenty of time for reading later.

'You coming to youth club with me tonight?' Peter asked as they sprawled on their stomachs in front of the

TV.

'Do I have to?' Ben said warily.

'No, I only asked.'

'What do you do?'

'Oh, all sorts. It depends. Tonight we're seeing a film.'

'What film?'

'It's about these missionary people in Bangladesh.'

Ben didn't have a clue where Bangladesh was, but the missionary bit sounded boring.

'Do you say prayers?' he asked.

'Yes, at the end.'

'Bor . . .ing!' Ben whistled.

Peter shook his head. 'No, it's not. We play pool, darts, table tennis or just listen to music. Then Mr Creedy shows us a film or talks about God. Sometimes we have people to talk to us. A policeman came in last time with his dog and gave us a demonstration. It was ace.'

Ben was doubtful. That was the only problem about being with the Thomases. Just as soon as you started to enjoy yourself they had to bring in God.

'Oh well, next time maybe?' Peter asked.

'Might,' Ben said. He was quite sure he'd never want to go to anything remotely associated with church but when Peter left at half-past six Ben felt half sorry that he hadn't said he'd go. For one thing, he was a bit curious about the youth club and, though he hated to admit it, he felt a bit lonely when Peter was gone.

Chapter Four

Ben didn't usually listen at doors to other people's conversations but on this occasion he couldn't help himself. It was a Saturday and they had all stayed in bed late. Mr and Mrs Thomas were getting breakfast ready and talking rather loudly, probably thinking the boys were still upstairs. Ben had his hand on the door knob when he heard Mrs Thomas say, 'Well let's just give it a couple of days and if you're still unhappy back he goes.'

Ben stopped in the hallway, trying to take in what he'd just heard. Did they mean him?

'There's the mess to be considered,' Mr Thomas was grumbling.

'Oh, that's a matter of training.'

Ben was astounded. He tried to think of the state he'd left his room in. Was it in such an awful mess that Mr Thomas was fed up? He'd thought Mr Thomas quite liked him.

'Getting under your feet,' Mr Thomas continued.

'But so cute!' his wife countered.

'Biting the furniture!' Mr Thomas warned.

Biting the what? Ben began to feel a bit bewildered by this conversation. They could accuse him of a lot of things but biting the furniture wasn't one of them.

The door opened and Mrs Thomas with a frying pan in her hand was about to call up the stairs. Ben blushed at being discovered.

'Oh, you're here already! Good, come and sit down.'

Ben edged to his seat, trying not to get in Mr Thomas's way or under his feet as he put it.

'We've got something to tell you, Ben,' Mrs Thomas said.

'I'm going to tidy my room after breakfast,' Ben said quickly.

Mrs Thomas looked a bit nonplussed. 'Oh, fine!' She stared at him as if he might have had a touch of the sun.

Peter stumbled in, still in pyjamas, and yawned loudly.

'Too many late nights for you, lad,' his father commented.

'Yes, that'll have to stop if you're going to take on a new responsibility,' his mum said.

'What new responsibility?' Peter asked, perking up.

'Your mother's idea,' Mr Thomas said.

'Oh come on, you'll love him when he arrives.'

'Mum! What's going on?' Peter demanded.

Mrs Thomas paused to build up the suspense. 'Mrs Litchfield's bitch has had a litter of puppies and she can't get rid of the last one, so . . .'

'Ace!' Peter was jumping up and down.

Ben, whose brain was unravelling the mystery of the conversation he'd overheard, was a bit slower to cotton on. When he did, his excitement was equal to Peter's. Living at Havens, the idea of having a pet was just a dream which wasn't even worth considering. Lillie always said she couldn't be doing with animals *and* children. Next to cars though, Ben adored animals, and dogs more than anything.

'When can we go and get it?' Peter asked, stuffing toast into his mouth as he spoke.

'As soon as you're ready. Oh, did you want to tidy

your room first, Ben?'

Peter gave Ben a similar 'Are you feeling OK?' look to the one his mum had given.

'Er, it can wait,' Ben mumbled, blushing.

'One condition – well, several actually,' Mr Thomas continued.

'For a start, if you two don't pull your weight with feeding, walking, etcetera he goes and he goes in any case if he causes too much havoc!'

Peter was quick to promise and Ben found himself volunteering as walker after school every weekday. As soon as the words were out of his mouth he remembered that he wasn't intending to be here in September in any case, and the thought was slightly depressing. Still, he could make the most of the puppy until then.

It seemed as if Mrs Thomas would never get ready but eventually she phoned Mrs Litchfield who said they could come over right away.

'What sort of dog is it?' Peter wanted to know as they drove the short distance to Mrs Litchfield's house.

'Well, Lulu is a labrador and the father was a collie so it should be a medium sized dog with a nice nature,' Mrs Thomas said.

'What colour, and what sex is it?' Peter continued.

'Black, I think she said, and it's a he.'

'Brilliant!'

As soon as the car stopped outside Mrs Litchfield's rambling gardens, the boys tumbled out and raced up to the front gate.

'Come on, Mum!' Peter urged.

'I'm coming – now don't get the puppies too excited.'

Mrs Litchfield was a large lady with bushy hair escaping from a headscarf, and she wore men's overalls.

'This way!' she called and led them straight through the house into a conservatory. The floor was covered in crumpled up newspaper.

Lulu was lying like a queen in a wicker basket while three puppies sprawled around her, their tiny claws scraping at the paper. They let out tiny high-pitched yelps as soon as the humans entered and Lulu raised her head wearily.

'The others went yesterday,' Mrs Litchfield explained, 'And a good thing too, eh old girl?' she murmured, giving Lulu a pat. 'They've worried the life out of her this past week! Now, here's the fellow who's looking for a home.'

She reached down to pick up the smallest of the three puppies who was trying to bite one of Lulu's ears.

'Is he big enough to leave his mother?' Mrs Thomas asked, doubtfully.

'To tell the truth, Lulu's milk is almost dried up, and he's always been the smallest. He'll do better away from her. A few raw eggs in milk and you'll see him put the weight on. Nothing wrong with him.'

'Oh no, I'm sure he's healthy,' Mrs Thomas said quickly, afraid in case she'd offended the woman.

'Now, I'm sorry I haven't quite got round to his inoculations yet, but I'm sure you can manage to arrange that?'

'Oh yes.'

'And don't let him out of the house or garden until you've got them done. Nasty kind of dog flu around, so it's best to keep him out of the way of any infection.

Mrs Thomas wondered what her husband would say about vet's bills for injections. The boys were practically inside the basket with Lulu trying to get a better look at the puppies.

'Now I don't want anything for him seeing as I know he's going to a good home,' Mrs Litchfield continued, 'but you do appreciate that I can't really be taking any

44

responsibility once he's gone?'

Mrs Thomas understood perfectly; there wouldn't be any trial period. Once they took the puppy he was their problem. She bit her lip uncertainly, but Ben looked up at her with such pleading eyes that any 'sensible' thoughts deserted her.

'Fine, we'll take him!'

'Lovely, I'm sure he'll make a good pet. Like I say, plenty of eggs and milk will do him wonders.'

Lulu, who looked as if she had a headache, didn't even glance up as they departed with her smallest puppy. Ben sympathised with the little black bundle of wet nose and fur. He knew how it felt not to be wanted.

Mrs Thomas, who'd forgotten to bring a box with them, put the puppy on Peter's lap with instructions not to let him *do* anything on the car seat. The excitement must have been too much however, because he *did* do something, all down the front of Peter's denim jacket.

'Ugh, mum!' Peter called, holding the puppy at arm's length.

Mrs Thomas glanced in the rear view mirror and sighed.

'Don't tell your father! I think he imagines this puppy is already house-trained. We'll let him discover otherwise in his own good time.'

'He needs a name,' Peter said as they lay on their stomachs playing with the puppy in the back garden that afternoon. Small or not, he was a plucky little fellow. One soft foam ball had already been shredded by his needle-sharp teeth and he was eyeing up Peter's best leather football with definite interest. Ben watched him bite the head off a dandelion flower with amusement.

'It ought to be a name which fits his character.'

'Hm, something brave and tough you mean?' Peter

said.

They laughed as the puppy sprang towards Tiggy, the next door neighbour's cat. She waved her tail majestically and then shot through the hedge with a screech.

'Hey, I know, we could call him Dan, after Daniel in the lion's den.'

'Who's he?' Ben asked.

'You know, in the Bible story – the one who gets thrown to the lions but they don't touch him.'

Ben rolled over, interested. 'That's a story in the Bible?' he asked, surprised.

'Yeah, it's really good.'

'Go on then.'

'What?'

'Tell me why he gets put in the lion's den.'

'Oh, this king throws him in there because he won't stop worshipping God. Everyone expects he's going to get eaten alive only he doesn't. He prays to God and the lions don't touch him.'

'So what does the king do?'

'He lets Daniel carry on praying to God – in fact he decides to as well.'

Ben thought about this for a while.

'Do you believe in all that?'

'Yes, of course. I mean the Bible is ever so old and if it wasn't true people wouldn't still be reading it and talking about God, would they?'

Ben didn't know.

'What about all this praying to God, then? Does it work?'

'Yes, I think so.'

'So if I prayed for something like this Daniel did, it would come true?'

'Well, not exactly.'

'Huh!' Ben said, as if that proved his point.

'It's not just like making a wish and it all comes true. You have to ask for help, to do something which God wants you to do. Like when you were trying to swim, I really prayed that you'd be able to make that width and you did.'

'Yeah, but that wasn't God, it was me. I'd have done it anyway,' Ben argued.

'That's what people who don't pray always say, but I think God helped me to teach you.'

Ben wasn't convinced. Still, he quite liked the sound of this Daniel bloke – and the way Tiggy had been sent off, it sort of fitted.

'Dan, then?' he said, tickling the puppy's limp velvety ear.

'Dan it is!' agreed Peter.

The puppy put its head on one side, as if it didn't care what it was being called.

'Are there any more stories like that Daniel one?' Ben asked, later.

'Hundreds. I've got this picture cartoon book with them all in. Do you want to borrow it? I'll put it on your bed tonight.'

'Yeah, ta,' Ben said. He must be going soft, wanting to read Bible stories. Still, if they weren't going to be soppy that was different.

'I suppose that's the last I'll see of you in the workshop for a while?' Mr Thomas grinned, as he joined the boys on the lawn.

'Oh no,' Ben said. 'I've already done that carburettor. Shall I go and get it?'

'Sure, let's see.'

'When have you been doing this?' Peter asked, as Ben returned with the shiny piece of metal.

'Oh, spare minutes.'

'Crikey, it's like new,' Peter enthused.

Mr Thomas turned it around in his hand gravely, inspecting it from every angle.

'That's an excellent bit of work, Ben. I couldn't have rubbed that down any better myself. We'll have to put you on to something more important next.'

Ben glowed with pleasure. If Mr Thomas thought it was good, then it *must* be, because he was a real expert.

Peter was looking at Ben with new eyes. He wasn't just the duffer who had to be helped along with everything – he had some pretty amazing skills all of his own.

'How do you get it to look like that?' Peter asked.

'It just takes time really,' Ben said modestly.

Peter inspected the object enviously. Patience was one skill he'd never had. He wished he'd shown a bit more interest in his dad's hobby now.

'There's a veteran car auction coming up in Cadmouth at the end of August,' Mr Thomas continued. 'I thought you and I could go, Ben. You never know, we might find an original hub to fit that offside wheel.'

'Brilliant, I'd love to go,' Ben said.

'Good, and I've got something for you,' Mr Thomas added. 'Wait a minute.'

He returned with a carrier bag which he passed to Ben. Inside was a pair of proper mechanic's overalls, with Ferrari badges and logos on each of the breast pockets. Ben held them up shyly. They were just the right length.

'Try them on,' Peter said.

Ben climbed into them, drawing the zip up to his throat.

'Bit baggy,' Peter commented, parading round him.

'They're supposed to be!' Mr Thomas laughed. 'Well, what do you think?' he added.

'Brilliant,' was all Ben could get out. He really felt the

part now and despite the fact that it was a sweltering day, he kept them on over his jeans for the rest of the afternoon.

Just before tea, Peter's aunt came over to visit. She was Mrs Thomas's sister and looked a bit like her but she was louder and brisker in her manner. She plonked herself down in a deckchair and watched the boys playing with Dan. She laughed at his antics until he tried to sink his teeth into her leather handbag.

'Little monster, get away!' she cried and took a swipe at him with a rolled up newspaper.

'Oh Aunt Jo, he's only little!' Peter protested.

'Never too young to learn!' Aunt Jo returned. 'And how are you getting on, Ben?' she asked, turning on him abruptly.

'OK, thanks,' Ben mumbled shyly.

'Good. Peter been introducing you to his friends yet?'

'Well . . .'

'Why not?' Aunt Jo wanted to know.

'Ben doesn't want to go to youth club and being on holiday, I've not seen much of my mates from school,' Peter explained.

'Why don't you want to go to youth club, Ben?'

He shrugged uncomfortably. 'I'm not that keen on church and things.'

Aunt Jo snorted. 'Goodness me. Well, at least you're honest, lad. What don't you like about it?'

'Well, I haven't actually gone yet.'

'Haven't gone and you say you don't like it? How can you tell?'

Ben had to shake his head. He wasn't up to this woman's sense of logic.

'When's that outing, Peter? The one you were telling me about.'

'On Monday. I'm not sure if I'm going. I mean, if Ben doesn't want to we might go swimming again.'

'Where is this trip?'

'It's to Acton Park.'

'What's that?'

'A huge fun-fair with incredible rides. It's supposed to have the longest logflume in Europe. You go over all these rapids in this rubber boat which spins you round and round. Then there's the corkscrew which flips you upside down in the seat and . . .'

'Enough!' Aunt Jo interrupted. 'It sounds absolutely revolting. I thank my lucky stars they weren't around when I was a child. Doesn't it sound awful, Ben?'

Ben looked at her warily. 'Sounds like it would be fun,' he finally said.

'Well, then! Why not go along and give it a try?'

'They'd all be people from youth club – I wouldn't know anyone,' Ben squirmed.

'Nonsense! You'd be with Peter anyway. Go on, give them a chance to get to know you. Then tell me whether they're all as daft as you think they are going to be!'

Aunt Jo was right – that was exactly what he was thinking.

'If I go on Monday, do I have to go every week?' Ben asked.

'Course not,' Peter answered him. 'We're allowed to bring friends on Monday anyway so there'll be other kids who don't always go to the club.'

'Well . . .'

'Oh, go on – it'll be fun!' Aunt Jo persuaded.

Ben wavered. He wasn't going to speak to anyone or do any daft singing but if it was just the park and then home it might be OK.

'All right,' he said at last.

'And you can spend this while you're there,' Aunt Jo

said. She took out her purse and gave the boys three pounds each. Ben had never had quite so much money to spend all in one go. He closed his hand around the hard coins feeling that he was holding a fortune.

'Coo, thanks Aunt Jo,' Peter said. 'I'm going to phone Mr Pritchard and tell him we're going. I hope there's still room on the coach.'

Chapter Five

As soon as Peter found out there were still spaces on the coach, the visit to Acton Park became his main topic of conversation. It was obvious, thought Ben, that Peter had missed spending more time with his friends this holiday and was bored with his company. Ben kept telling himself that it didn't matter but, for the first time in his life, he felt jealous. It was daft, of course, because he had no intention of staying with the Thomas family after the end of August anyway but he couldn't help resenting it when Peter phoned up a mate from school to ask if *he* was going too.

Ben was also a bit worried about meeting a load of new kids. There had always been kids coming and going at Havens but *there* everyone was in the same boat and you didn't have to pretend. Here, they would be curious about who he was and where from, unless they already knew, in which case they'd probably treat him like some charity kid and stare. Worst of all they'd be Christians. The more Ben thought about this, the less he looked forward to the trip. If only Aunt Jo hadn't persuaded him. Well, he wasn't going to be nice to *anyone,* then they'd leave him alone. He didn't care whether they were Peter's friends or not. For all he cared, Peter could go off and leave him. He didn't need anyone. With any luck it would rain on them and they'd get their soppy

Bibles wet.

Monday arrived warm, dry and sunny, however, Mrs Thomas packed masses of sandwiches and homemade biscuits, just to keep them going, she said, and drove them to the church in plenty of time for the departure. Knots of kids were already drifting along the road towards St. Giles, and some were sitting on the church wall as they pulled up.

'Look after Dan,' Peter said as he got out of the car.

'Will do – it's his inoculations this afternoon,' Mrs Thomas remembered.

'Bye, little fellow,' Ben said, tickling the puppy's nose affectionately. Dan immediately rolled over on his back, legs squirming in mid-air.

'I wish he could come too,' Peter sighed.

'Go on, you'll have a great time and Dan will be waiting when you get back. Now, have you got everything? Food, money, spare jumper . . .'

'Yes, Mum!' Peter interrupted.

'And you're all right, Ben?'

He nodded dumbly and Mrs Thomas frowned at him worriedly. She wished she understood him better but when he was quiet like this there was just no getting through to him.

'I'll pick you up at seven o'clock, then. Be good.'

Ben gave Dan one more pat and then reluctantly slid out of the car. The little dog went frantic when he realised he wasn't going with them, his paws scrabbling at the door. As Mrs Thomas pulled away they watched a black nose pressed against the window.

'Ah, maybe we can get him a new toy today with our pocket money,' Peter said.

'Yeah, let's,' Ben agreed. 'I hope his injections won't hurt.'

'It's for his own good, though, and it means we can

take him out for proper walks once they're done.'

With this prospect in mind, Ben trotted towards the kids now scrambling to get on the coach, feeling only moderately bolshy.

'Hi Kev, this is Ben,' Peter said as soon as they joined the queue. 'Hey, bag us two seats near the back,' he shouted to a girl with a pony-tail just getting on.

'OK, if I can,' she shouted back.

Everyone seemed to be talking at once and Peter was telling him names so fast that Ben gave up and just kept grinning when people said hello to him. They were all friendly, he noticed, and nobody was staring at him. Still, they were too busy squashing on the coach.

'Steady there!' a loud voice boomed in Ben's ear.

'That's Brian,' Peter said, nudging Ben in the ribs. 'He's one of our youth club leaders.'

Brian took command and soon had the queue in some kind of line so everyone could get on more quickly. Another man got on and started to count people and a woman in a bright yellow dress gave instructions about what to do if you felt travel sick.

The girl with the pony-tail had saved Peter two seats on the back row. It was a bit squashed but once they'd stowed their bags on the shelf it was OK.

'Shift up, Ben, then Kev can sit by you,' Peter instructed.

Ben moved up reluctantly and Kev plonked himself down. Ben felt his lip curl. Kev was a right soft weed. He had curls like a girl and wore glasses which he kept pushing up his nose with his middle finger. A typical Christian, Ben thought.

As soon as the coach starts, I bet they'll all be singing hymns and clapping, Ben thought in disgust, but he was wrong. The coach driver had a microphone to speak into. He was really funny and told them one or two jokes as they drove out of Cadmouth. Then he said if anyone wanted to listen to music they could pass their cassettes forward and he'd play them over his stereo system. Lots of kids had Walkmans and they sent cassettes forward.

'Here, I've brought a couple of tapes,' Kev said, unzipping his bag. 'What do you like?' he asked, dropping them into Ben's lap.

Ben read the labels. One was Heavy Metal which he didn't much care for, the other was Yello, which he was mad about. Neither were the sort of music he'd expected Kev to like.

'This is pretty good,' he said.

'OK. Here, Sally, shove this one forward. Ta.' Kev handed the tape to a ginger-haired girl.

Ben settled back. They'd joined the motorway northbound and there hadn't been a single chorus yet. They were still soppy, though.

It was a long journey but they stopped at the service station about eleven o'clock and then, Peter said, they'd only got about another hour to go.

Peter was pretty popular, Ben could tell. But then, they all seemed to know each other and the chattering never stopped. Brian came down to say hello to everyone on the coach. He shook hands with Ben in a very grown-up way and said how pleased he was to meet him and how he hoped to see him at youth club. Ben didn't reply. They'd be asking him to church next.

Then they caught sight of signs for Acton Park and people stopped chattering to watch out for the next one.

'It'll be brilliant!' Peter was saying. 'We'll go on the log flume first, Kev.' He seemed to have forgotten Ben.

They pulled up in a vast car park and once off the coach, filed through turnstiles into the park. The whole place was enclosed so once you were in, you could wander anywhere quite safely and all the rides were free.

'We're going to eat lunch together first,' Brian said, ushering them all into the shade under some chestnut trees. There were about thirty-five kids and they spread themselves in a huge lop-sided circle on the grass.

'Let's say grace,' Brian said, when everyone was still. He repeated words which were familiar to Ben by now and thirty-four voices chanted 'Amen' at the end. Ben kept his mouth tightly closed. Fancy praying in a park!

'I think it's daft saying thanks to God for food when everyone knows their mums made the sandwiches,' Ben muttered as he bit into a cheese and pickle one.

Kev nodded. 'Yes, I used to think that till my dad explained it.'

Ben glanced at him curiously. 'Well, how did he explain it then?'

'You just go back a few steps. Your mum makes the sandwiches say, but the baker has to have the flour first, and that's up to the farmer. Only he has to have the land and rain to make crops grow.'

'And the rain is just free,' Ben said, following his train of thought, 'so we needn't say thank you at all.'

'But the rain and soil and the seed are there because someone made them. People didn't, so it must be God. If we didn't have seeds and animals we'd die, so we're thanking him for giving us the things we need to keep us alive and comfortable,' Kev explained. 'Do you see?'

Ben was rather taken aback by Kev's simple logic. 'I suppose so,' he admitted. He'd have to think about it at home, Ben decided. He looked at Kev with rather different thoughts than he'd had earlier. Perhaps the kid wasn't quite such a wimp after all.

'At least the bag'll be a bit lighter once we've eaten some of this,' Peter said, tossing an apple in Ben's direction.

'Now, everyone is to meet back at the turnstiles at four o'clock. We'll be at the turnstiles every hour, in case any one needs us, and Mrs Parr will be in the children's zoo area all afternoon. If you get lost just make your way there – it's the easiest place to recognise. Off you go, and enjoy yourselves!' Brian waved them away.

With shouts and laughter the circle of children broke up and scattered.

Kev, Peter, Ben and a boy called Alan made for the log flume. There was quite a queue but as it weaved in and out of bollards you never had to stand still for long. When they were in sight of the artificial rapids, they could hear squeals as people were soaked under water jets. Ben felt his mouth go dry with excitement. He'd only ever seen this sort of thing on TV.

Suddenly they were at the head of the queue. An attendant grabbed him under the arms and lifted him into the rubber dinghy, then helped him fasten a tough belt around his waist. Peter and Kev were on either side of him. Alan joined others in another boat and then they were off. Slowly at first, the channel of water bobbed them along in the raised metal trough. They joined a wider stretch of water and then the ride really began. The dinghy hovered on the edge of a precipice then shot over into a boiling mass of bubbling water. The stomach-lurching drop left Ben's voice about two foot above his head and by the time it caught up, his screams were swallowed by the roar of a waterfall which shot jets of freezing water into their faces and down their backs. Ben dug his nails into the holding bar as they did a double turn and skimmed over some very real looking rocks. His teeth rattled in his head. Peter was mouthing words at him but he couldn't hear anything. Kev grabbed his arm and pointed to a grotesque crocodile monster which leered at them from a slimy cave as they swept past. Ben was terrified and excited at the same time. It was a brilliant ride – better than anything he'd ever been on. The climax was a drop of about six feet, which felt like sixty, and the jolt as they hit the water reverberated up their spines. All too soon, their sturdy craft was towed into the side and attendants helped them out. They passed some gates and were back in the park, the thunder of water still ringing in their ears.

'What did I tell you?' Peter cried. 'Wasn't it ace?'

Ben nodded, breathless and too wobbly on his feet to walk properly.

'Come on, let's try the corkscrew!' Kev was saying.

Unfortunately you had to be a certain height to go on this ride, which turned you upside down in a car on rails. A bar at the entrance indicated how high you had to be and since neither Alan nor Ben reached it, they abandoned the idea.

'We'll do it next year,' Peter promised as they raced off to the dodgems. Four hours had seemed a long time but minutes raced by as they scampered from ride to ride. They had two more goes on the log flume, several goes on the dodgems, a go on the human wheel which nearly made Kev sick and then a go on the big wheel.

'I'm hot,' Alan said at last. 'Let's go and buy a drink.'

Ben was glad to follow them. His stomach didn't quite feel as if it belonged to him anymore. He decided candy-floss would hold it down. If anything it did the opposite. Then they sat at tables drinking Coke and planned their last hour.

'We need to find the shops,' Peter explained, 'so we can buy a present for Dan.'

'Who's Dan?' Kev asked.

'My new puppy,' Peter boasted. 'Well, ours really,' he added as he caught Ben's eye.

'Get on! What's he like?'

'He's cute, but he eats balls for breakfast.'

'You want to get him one of those plastic ones with a bell inside. Our cat loves it.'

'Well, maybe. What do you think, Ben?' Peter asked. Ben shrugged.

'I want another go on the skittles alley,' said Alan. 'You coming?'

'I will. See you two later,' Kev called.

Ben sucked up the last of his Coke and belched loudly.

Peter got up. 'Come on, let's find the shop.'

There were several gift shops near the café, some selling pottery and china, others selling plants, skirts and gaudy framed pictures. The boys ignored these and headed straight for the toy shop. Ben stared at the display of model cars with big eyes but dutifully dragged himself away. Dan needed a present first.

'Here, there's this,' Peter said, picking up a ball with eyes that swivelled, set into it.

'He'll break it in no time,' Ben said.

'True.'

'This is a good one.' Ben reached up to a high shelf and picked up a ball similar to the one Alan had described. Instead of a bell, it squeaked when you pressed it.

'He'll love it! How much is it?'

They checked the price tag and were dismayed to discover it cost two pounds fifty.

'What have we got between us?' Peter said.

They had both spent over a pound each on drink, candyfloss and sweets. Ben had one pound fifty left, Peter had one pound ninety.

'Well, we could do it, but it doesn't leave us much.'

Ben glanced back at the model cars. They had a BMW Corgi there for one pound forty-five. He could have afforded it, but not if Dan was to get his present. He wished he hadn't bought the candy-floss – especially as it had been horrible really. It was then that the idea struck him.

'I know, we'll get the ball in a minute, and I can promise we'll still have some money left over. Come on.'

Peter followed him back to the café beside which Ben pointed to a one-armed bandit arcade.

'You're not going in there, are you?' Peter said.

'Course. Steve back at Havens played them all the time. He said it paid for his luxuries.'

'I don't believe that! Anyway, you're not old enough to play on them, it's illegal. Besides, you'll just lose all your money.'

'Rubbish – if you put enough in you're bound to get some back.'

'Not necessarily – you could just lose the lot.'

'I won't. If you gave me yours as well I'd be doubly sure of making a profit.'

'No way,' said Peter putting his money firmly in his pocket.

'Chicken!' Ben taunted.

'Don't go in there,' Peter warned.

'Gonna stop me?' Ben snarled, getting aggressive now that Peter was so adamant.

'Brian wouldn't like it,' Peter pleaded.

'Huh, so what! I'm not fussed about him.'

'Well, I'm not coming with you. And if you get caught it's your tough luck.'

'Ah, go and say your prayers!' Ben threw back as he stalked into the arcade. He knew he was being horrible but he felt cross with Peter. Once he'd won something, a fiver say, Peter would be patting him on the back. He'd show him.

In the gloomy room, only the lurid lights of the machines flashed and buzzed. Ben stared at them hesitantly, clasping the warm coins in his hand. He'd never actually played on his own, only pushed buttons for Steve a couple of times. Steve had always seemed to win.

At last he selected a machine and, glancing around first, pushed fifty pence into the slot. It fell with a dead clank and numbers lit up. Ben pushed the red button and lines of fruit flipped over in front of his eyes. Nothing matched. He stabbed at the button again. Nothing. Again. Nothing. Licking his dry lips, Ben drummed his fingers on the glass front, willing the cherries or the apples to group together. Two more goes and his money was gone. Ben stared at the pound coin. Could he chance it, or should he walk away? The flickering lights tempted him. Pictures of coins sparkled in front of his eyes. He desperately pushed in the coin in his hand. Be bold, Steve had once said. Well, he'd gambled everything now. The machine *had* to pay him back.

It didn't. Less than two minutes later, Ben walked out of the arcade penniless. The place in his hand where the coin had dug in felt horribly cold and empty. Sunlight made him squint. Peter was leaning against the wall of the arcade. He looked at Ben and knew.

'You lost it all, didn't you? Huh! Great! So now Dan doesn't get his ball *and* you don't get your model car. I *told* you so!' he added as if he just couldn't help himself saying it.

Ben scowled. He felt close to tears.

'Yeah, you're such a goody-goody superman. I bet you've never done anything wrong in your life!'

'That's not fair!'

Ben knew it wasn't, and he felt even worse. He hated himself, and Peter and the stupid trip. He'd spoiled everything.

It was a miserable journey home. They stopped at a service station for tea and Ben stayed on the coach. Peter left him there. He returned with a packet of chips.

'Want one?' he asked, rather ungraciously.

'No!' Ben replied viciously.

'Fair enough,' Peter turned away and ate the chips without another word.

Chapter Six

Mrs Thomas didn't know what had happened on the trip to Acton Park. She could only assume it was something important from the fact that Peter and Ben still weren't talking to each other by Tuesday afternoon. Peter spent the entire morning kicking a football against the dustbin until his mum thought she would go mad, and Ben slunk off to the workshop, closing the door very firmly behind him. Dan added to Mrs Thomas's annoyance by twice wetting the kitchen floor, and was banished to the garden.

At lunch time Mrs Thomas tried to coax Peter into making it up with Ben but Peter wasn't to be moved.

'It's not *me* who's in a mood, it's *him*. I tried talking to him this morning and he just ignored me. Anyway it's his problem not mine, it wasn't me who . . .' Peter trailed off, unwilling to say any more.

Ben wandered in just then and instinctively knew they'd been talking about him. He bristled with anger. No doubt Peter's mum was going to give him a lecture now on the dangers of gambling. Well, just let her try!

'Toast under your beans or bread?' Mrs Thomas asked, smiling at him.

Ben glanced sideways at Peter. Perhaps he hadn't landed him in it after all. He still had that superior nose-in-the-air look, though. Ben had once sent a girl at

Havens to Coventry for two whole weeks so ignoring Peter until at least the weekend would be no problem.

He bit into a slice of toast tastelessly and found he had quite a job swallowing it. Peter didn't seem to have lost his appetite.

'What about swimming this afternoon?' Mrs Thomas suggested brightly, as they washed up.

'No, thanks,' came simultaneously from both boys.

'Oh. Well, what about coming to the shops with me?'

'Ben can go, I want to stay here and practise my goal shots,' Peter said.

Ben hated being spoken for like that, as if he was some kind of package to be passed around.

'How about it, Ben?' Mrs Thomas asked.

'I'd rather stay here.'

'All right, we'll all stay in and I'll get on with some baking.'

Mrs Thomas carefully balanced two glass tumblers on top of each other to drain. Ben reached for one but the suction caused by the water stuck the other one to it.

'Watch out!' Peter called but it was too late. Suddenly giving way, the tumbler underneath bounced once on the edge of the sink, chipping, then smashed on the floor projecting fragments of glass in all directions. Ben stood surrounded by bits of debris with his mouth open. He couldn't have done a more effective demolition job on the tumbler if he'd aimed it at a brick wall.

Mrs Thomas was all apologies, as she bent down to pick up the biggest pieces.

'Stupid thing of me to do, I'm sorry, love. You haven't cut yourself, have you? Here, step over there while I sweep up.'

Ben felt clumsy and stupid and when he caught sight of Peter's grinning face he automatically assumed he was being laughed at. He dropped the tea-towel and stalked out.

'What *is* the matter with the boy?' Mrs Thomas sighed as the door slammed behind him.

'Don't worry, he'll get over it,' Peter said calmly.

'You could have made a bit more effort this lunch time.'

'Oh, mum . . .' Peter groaned.

'No, Peter. You think about it. Whatever happened between you yesterday, this has gone on too long.'

'It's up to him to make an effort as well.'

'That's not what we've tried to teach you, Peter,' his mum reminded him as she flung glass in the bin. 'It isn't easy for Ben being here, you know. There are bound to be problems getting used to each other and he's obviously upset about this row you've had.'

'He doesn't care at all!' Peter protested.

'Of course he does! Why do you think he's keeping out of our way and sulking off like that?'

Peter stopped kicking the edge of the table leg with his toe and thought about this.

'I didn't upset him, he upset himself.'

'Maybe, but you could still try to help him by being friendly.'

'Why should I? You saw what he's like.'

'We can't just be nice to people who are nice back. Remember what Jesus said about treating people as we would like them to treat *us*. Put yourself in Ben's position and see how he feels.'

Peter had a twinge of conscience about the 'I told you so'. He couldn't stand it when people said that to him. He *had* offered to share his chips, he remembered, but when he thought about how pompous he'd felt when he offered them he squirmed inside. Ben had learnt his lesson about gambling machines on his own yesterday. If only he had been more understanding

65

about it instead of nagging him and making him feel small, they wouldn't be at loggerheads now.

'Go and play football, then,' Mrs Thomas said wearily.

'Yeah. Hey mum, perhaps I'll go and see what Ben's doing in the workshop later.'

Mrs Thomas smiled. 'Good.'

Feeling much better now that he'd made up his mind to be friends again, Peter decided to spend just half an hour on goal shots and then he'd take Ben a biscuit and make up. His first shot was dead centre.

Ben stood in the workshop fuming with anger and not knowing who or what to take it out on. He picked up a can of cleaning spirit and tipped a little into a jam jar. He was rubbing down an old rusty panel and it was going to be a long job. The morning's efforts looked insignificant when he thought how much more needed to be done. Usually Ben would have ploughed on patiently but this afternoon he felt too frustrated. He suddenly had an idea for speeding up the process. If he sprinkled the spirit all over the panel, it would be loosening up the dirt and rust before he got to it with the sandpaper and rags.

Pleased with his plan, Ben reached for the can. It had a plastic lip which helped pouring but it swivelled to face downwards no matter what angle it was held at. The two litre can was quite heavy and it was a bit slippery. Just as Ben raised the can to waist level and began tipping, the can swivelled, pouring a stream of fluid down his trouser leg and filling his left shoe. Ben jerked backwards, the spout shot out of the can and the rest of the liquid spurted out into a puddle on the floor.

He managed to save about a cupful in the bottom of the can, the rest was wasted. It was expensive stuff, Mr Thomas had once told him, and that was why you used it sparingly from a jam jar. Ben tried to imagine explaining how he'd had this good idea for washing the workshop floor and his overalls in cleaning spirit but he couldn't. All he could imagine was Mr Thomas's reaction.

He couldn't do anything to make the mess look better and he certainly couldn't go into the house until his trouser leg dried off or Mrs Thomas would want to know what it was.

Ben squelched outside wishing he'd never bothered to get up that morning. It was one of those days. If only Ben had thought about that for long enough he might not have followed up his second 'good' idea of the day. As he emerged into the sunlight, Dan, who'd been chewing an old shoe on the lawn, scampered up to him, sniffing curiously at the wet shoe.

'Hello, Dan,' Ben sighed, stooping down to pat him and have his face licked. 'At least *you're* still my friend.'

As if to prove it, Dan rolled over on his back to have his tummy tickled.

'I bet you'd love to go out, wouldn't you?' Ben murmured.

The puppy bit his hand playfully, asking to be chased.

'Come on, we're going out – just you and me.'

Ben crept to the back door and listened. There was no-one in the kitchen. All he could hear was Peter's football thudding against the side wall of the house.

Ben slipped inside, took Dan's brand new red lead and collar and dashed back to where the puppy had retrieved his shoe.

'Come on, sit still a minute,' Ben commanded, trying to fix the collar on, but Dan just thought it was a new game and tried to chew the buckle whenever it came near his mouth.

After a considerable struggle, Ben managed to fasten the collar but Dan wasn't at all sure about this. He wriggled and backed away, then leapt at the lead until he'd got it between his teeth.

Ben dragged him on his bottom for several yards before Dan got the hang of walking in a straight line but it wasn't a bit like the dog walking that Ben had watched people do in the park.

They managed to get to the end of the road but then had to stop while Ben untied the lead from around Dan's back legs.

'Come on, boy!' Ben urged, as the puppy suddenly took it into his head to sit down on the pavement and watch a passing butterfly, but Dan wouldn't budge. In the end Ben tucked him under his arm and carried him as far as the recreation ground. Once there he put him down again, at which point Dan shot sideways. He caught sight of another dog and was keen to investigate. Ben had no option but to follow.

'This is useless, you daft dog!' Ben cried later as Dan rolled over on his back winding the lead twice round his barrel-like body. 'I know what you'd like – a run without the lead. Come on, then, let's unclip the buckle.'

Ben knelt down on the soft grass to undo the lead but Dan was too impatient. He put his head down, wriggled his neck and escaped from collar and lead in one go.

'Oh, come here!' Ben shouted, holding the limp leather collar.

Free at last, Dan had no intention of being made a prisoner again. He hadn't thought much of being tied to a boy who didn't move where *he* wanted to. Keeping well beyond arm's reach he capered across the recreation ground towards the road.

At first, Ben laughed as he followed him, making dives every now and then but always missing. It wasn't until they were quite close to the main road that he began to be seriously worried.

'Dan! Come back! Stop!' he shouted.

But the dog, hugely enjoying his game of tag, only ran faster, not even stopping to yelp as he had been doing.

Ben stopped calling and concentrated on running but four legs had a huge advantage over his two. If only Peter was here to head him off. Feeling sick, Ben watched the puppy dart across the road, narrowly missing the wheels of a car whose driver hooted angrily. The noise frightened Dan, who streaked away, round a corner and out of sight.

Ben followed but he had to wait for a gap in the traffic and this gave the puppy a head start. Almost sobbing with fear, Ben pounded up the road in the direction Dan had sprinted. When he reached the corner there was no sight of the puppy.

'Oh Dan, please wait, please don't get run over,' Ben gasped as he belted along the pavements. When the stitch in his side finally creased him in two, he paused, hands on his knees trying to get air into his burning lungs.

As soon as he'd recovered he carried on, running and walking, but with every step less convinced that he was going in the right direction. Dan could have doubled back, could have got into someone's garden. He was only little. He'd want to have a rest soon. Maybe he'd gone home – taken a short cut. But then Ben remembered that he'd never been out of the garden before. How would he possibly know where home was? Were dogs like homing pigeons, Ben wondered, trying to remember nature lessons at school. He didn't think so.

He was almost lost himself by the time he decided to give up. They'd be having tea at home. Mr Thomas would be back, so he'd have discovered the spilt fluid. What a mess. Ben wished he could walk to Havens. He didn't know how he was going to face the Thomases. Telling Peter he'd lost Dan. This would be the worst moment in his life.

Not hurrying, because he didn't want to arrive, Ben trudged miserably back home.

Back at the Thomases, Peter couldn't believe the state his mum had worked herself into.

'He's run away. He's been kidnapped. Oh, what am I going to do?' she moaned, wringing her hands.

'Calm down!' Mr Thomas said, but even he had turned pale. 'I've phoned the police and they'll be keeping an eye out. He's probably got lost, or forgotten the time.'

'But he's been gone hours!'

Peter stared at his mum miserably. If only he'd told her why Ben had been in a mood, if only he'd followed him to the workshop right away . . .

'He's taken Dan, you say?' Mr Thomas said, trying to get the facts from his wife.

'Yes, yes. Oh my goodness, why didn't he say he was going? The dog shouldn't be out of the garden for another week anyway.'

'That's the least of our problems,' her husband said sensibly.

'Perhaps he thought I was cross about the glass, but I wasn't! I wasn't, Peter, was I?' Mrs Thomas wailed.

'I'm going to have a look myself. I'll take the car. You stay by the phone. Peter, make some tea.'

Peter obeyed, glad to have a reason to do something.

He had just plugged the kettle in when Ben walked through the back door, hands in his pockets.

Mrs Thomas yanked him across the room, patting him all over to check he was all right. 'Oh Ben!' she sighed, relief almost visibly pouring over her, but the next moment a strange reaction overtook her. It was a kind of anger that she'd been so unnecessarily concerned.

'What on earth did you think you were doing, running off like that?' she cried, shaking him slightly.

Mr Thomas joined in. 'Do you know the police are out looking for you? We've been worried sick.'

'I just went for a walk,' Ben tried to explain.

'But you're not *old* enough to wander off on your own. It was a very silly thing to do. Anything could have happened,' Mrs Thomas shouted.

Anything *did*, Ben thought wretchedly.

'Where's Dan?' Peter asked, as his parents stopped talking.

Ben raised tear-filled eyes to him. 'I've lost him,' he said quietly.

'You've *what?*' Peter screamed.

'His collar came off. I let him off,' Ben corrected. There was no point trying to make it sound better than it was.

'Where?' Peter said.

'In the recreation ground.'

'So where is he now?' Mr Thomas said, trying to catch up with developments.

'I tried to follow him but he ran too fast and now, I don't know where he is.'

'You idiot!' Peter cried, all his guilty feelings of concern evaporating. 'He wasn't even supposed to be out for walks yet.'

'But you said . . .'

'He hadn't been trained to the lead!' Mrs Thomas said. 'Oh Ben, how could you!'

'It wasn't my fault,' Ben pleaded, but he knew it was. Everything was his fault and they all hated him. A tear ran down his cheek, leaving a dirty trail.

'I'm going to look for him!' Peter flared.

'No, you are not!' his father said. 'One missing boy per day is quite enough. We'll eat tea, I'll phone the police and ask them to look out for a puppy, not a boy, and then we'll take a drive later on round the recreation ground.'

'I don't want tea,' Ben sniffed.

'Go and have a shower, Ben. I'll bring you up some tea later,' Mrs Thomas said. Her anger had vanished as quickly as it had appeared. Only Peter could ignore Ben's misery, and that was because he was equally upset over the missing puppy.

'What an awful smell!' Mr Thomas said, staring at Ben's stained trouser leg. Ben looked down at himself.

'Something else happened this afternoon . . .', he began.

Chapter Seven

Ben stayed in his room for the rest of the evening. He heard Mr Thomas and Peter go out in the car and a little later Mrs Thomas brought him up a tray of food. He looked at it hungrily but the thought of Dan alone somewhere, whimpering for *his* tea, put him off.

Mrs Thomas sat down beside him on the bed where Ben had been flicking absently through his car magazines.

'I'm sorry I shouted at you earlier,' she said.

'I deserved it,' he replied simply.

'You shouldn't have gone off on your own but losing Dan was an accident.'

'Peter's really upset, isn't he?'

'Yes, but the same thing could have happened to him.'

Ben doubted it. Peter would have had more sense, or at any rate he'd have run fast enough to keep up with Dan.

'I'm sorry I've caused so much trouble,' Ben paused, and then said the thing which had been on his mind while he'd been sitting alone. 'Will you want me to go back to Havens now?'

Mrs Thomas looked surprised. 'Why on earth should we?'

'Because I've lost Dan and made Peter cross.'

'But I've told you, it could just as easily have been Peter.'

'Yes, but he's your son and I'm just . . .'

'Oh Ben, I hoped we'd made you feel like a part of our family. You're just as important as Peter.'

'What about Mr Thomas?'

'He feels exactly the same way. Of course it's up to you in the end. I mean, this was just a trial and if you're not happy with us, then nobody will force you to stay.'

'It's not that,' Ben said quickly. He realised now something which had been in the back of his mind for quite a time. He really did like the Thomases. More than anything he wanted to stay and he wanted to be friends with Peter.

'If only they could find Dan,' Ben said miserably, as he rolled over on his stomach.

'Don't give up hope. Listen, I can hear the car. Maybe they've got him with them, and, if not, well someone is sure to return him before long.'

'But they won't know where he lives without a collar.'

'Most people would contact the police or the RSPCA if they found a stray dog, especially if it's a puppy.'

'I wish I could *do* something,' Ben said.

'You can pray that he's safe and being looked after tonight,' Mrs Thomas said quietly.

Ben looked up – it was the first time he'd ever been told to pray. He didn't know how. What did you say? Oh, it was silly anyway. I mean there wasn't a God to listen, was there? And even if there was, he didn't have time for boys like Ben who didn't go to church and who laughed at Christians.

'I'll go and see what news they've got. Are you coming down?'

Ben shook his head. He didn't feel up to facing Mr Thomas yet and definitely not Peter.

'We all love you, Ben, no matter what happens,' Mrs Thomas said as she stood at the door.

If only it were true, Ben thought. He couldn't remember anyone saying that to him before. It was soppy of course, but it gave him a slightly more comfortable feeling inside. He took a sandwich from the tray.

Ben knew they hadn't found Dan by the lack of noise downstairs. Mrs Thomas didn't come back up, so that meant there wasn't any good news. Worst of all, Ben was certain he could hear Peter crying before the lounge door closed on the sound. He ached with wretchedness. It was bad enough to have lost something you really cared about, but when it belonged to someone else as well, that made it doubly awful. In spite of Mrs Thomas's kind words it was plain to Ben that Peter would never forgive him and, if Dan was lost forever, there was no way he could stay. So it looked as if he'd be back at Havens after all, only for all the wrong reasons.

Ben was very surprised some time later when Peter came upstairs and knocked on his bedroom door. They stood staring at each other awkwardly for several seconds, wondering who was going to be brave enough to break the silence.

'Look, I'm sorry,' they both began at the same time.

Peter laughed weakly and Ben budged up on the bed so they could both sit down.

'It's all my fault. I don't expect you want to be friends again,' Ben stammered.

'Yes, I do. It's not *all* your fault. If I hadn't been so stuck up over the money we'd have gone swimming this afternoon and none of this would have happened. I'm sorry.'

'That's OK,' Ben said, feeling embarrassed. He was sure he deserved to be called an idiot again, not apologised to. 'Can we be mates again?' he asked shyly.

'Yeah, sure.'

'But what if . . .?'

'Don't say that. We're going to find him, we've just *got* to.'

Ben was silent, thinking things over.

'Dad's going to put an advert in the paper tomorrow,' Peter said, as cheerfully as he could. 'And we've phoned the RSPCA just in case someone brings him in. We've seen a few of the neighbours too and they've promised to keep an eye open.'

'What about Kev?' Ben suddenly remembered.

'Hey, yeah! He lives the other side of the recreation ground and he's always cycling round there with his older brother. Let's go and phone him now.'

Ben hesitated. 'Is your dad cross about the workshop?'

Peter grinned for the first time that evening.

'He was laughing about your face when you told him about that, all the way down the road.'

Ben shook his head. Adults never took the right things seriously. Go for a walk and they went barmy. Spill a load of expensive fluid and they laughed.

There was something else Ben needed to ask Peter.

'Have you prayed about Dan?' he said as casually as he could.

'Yes.'

'When?'

'Oh, as we were driving along, and when Dad went into the neighbour's house.'

'What did you say?'

'I asked God to help us find Dan, and not let him get run over.'

'Just like that?'

'Yes, of course.'

'But don't you have to have proper long sentences

76

to pray to God?' Ben asked, remembering a vicar who'd once taken an assembly for his class.

'It doesn't matter. Some prayers are complicated and long, others are quick and simple. Mine had to be short because there wasn't much time.'

'And do you reckon God listens?'

'Yes!' Peter said in a tone which meant there couldn't possibly be any doubt about it.

'Can *I* pray to God? I mean, I'm not a Christian or anything.'

'God wants everyone to know him. You have to talk to people if you want to get to know them. It's the same with God.'

'I suppose I do believe in God a bit,' Ben said.

'Well then, you're on the way to becoming a Christian. God will listen.'

'And answer?' Ben said hopefully.

'Yes, in the way that he thinks is best.'

'But you didn't find Dan, and you'd prayed you would,' Ben sighed.

'We didn't find him run over,' Peter pointed out, 'and I believe God can keep him safe tonight.'

'Shall I pray, too?' Ben asked, getting to the point at last.

'That's a good idea,' Peter said warmly.

'And I can just say anything?'

'Anything.'

Ben screwed his eyes up tightly and concentrated on Dan's face and the recreation ground. Please let Dan be somewhere safe tonight and let him have something to eat. Amen. Oh, and I'm sorry for losing him, he added.

Ben opened his eyes. He wished he'd asked God to let him stay here and to find Dan but as it was his first prayer he thought he ought not to ask for too much. If

Dan was kept safe until the morning that would be a great enough thing for God to do.

'Let's go and phone Kev,' Peter said.

Ben was still a bit wary of Mr Thomas at first but as there was no mention of his misdeed with the fluid he quickly relaxed.

In the lounge, Mr Thomas was outlining a plan of action for the morning. He had a street map of the town spread out on the table and had marked the recreation ground with a felt-tip pen.

'Now, Ben, show us where you last saw Dan.'

Ben peered at the maze of roads and wished he could read a map.

'It was the road with the cycle shop in,' he remembered.

'Good boy. That's Vernay Street. So, we can mark all the possible roads he might have followed after that. Now then,' Mr Thomas drew a thick black line down each road.

'As least there aren't any big open spaces that way,' Peter said.

'Of course he may have doubled back on himself but it's much more likely he'd have tired himself out and just flopped down on someone's front door step. So here's the plan. We split up tomorrow. I'll take one of you in the car and we'll knock on doors in streets north of the High Street. Pam, you take the other and go on foot down all the roads south. Agreed?'

The boys nodded. 'Can I go with you, Dad?' Peter asked.

'Fine. Now, off to bed, you lads. I've phoned the office to say I'm taking the morning off, so I can give you until lunch time. We'll aim to start knocking on doors at nine o'clock.'

Ben looked at Mr Thomas with admiration. Seeing as

he wasn't even that much of a dog lover, he was taking the whole thing really seriously and he hadn't said a word about how daft Ben had been.

He and Peter went off to bed in as cheerful a mood as could be expected under the circumstances.

The next morning was another clear sunny day, and it would be hot work trailing around houses. Mrs Thomas filled two bottles with squash for the boys and then they scrambled into the car. Mrs Thomas and Ben were dropped off first.

'Good luck!' Peter shouted as his mum and Ben set off down their first road. Ben watched Peter go reluctantly. On his own he felt all his confidence about the campaign melt away. Still, he had to try as hard as he could. Before knocking on the first door Ben closed his eyes and said a prayer. Please God, let one of us find Dan this morning, Amen. It was a very bold request, but it was the only thing Ben could think of. If they didn't find Dan today he couldn't imagine they'd ever see him again.

'You take the odd numbers, I'll take evens,' Mrs Thomas instructed.

Ben trotted up the first pathway, his hopes high. They were quickly dashed. After ten houses, he felt awful, the reply was always the same. No, they hadn't seen a black puppy but, yes, they'd keep an eye out.

Ben was infuriated by little deaf old ladies who didn't hear what he was saying.

'No, I don't take a daily paper,' one old lady said.

'No, puppy!' Ben repeated.

'Puppy? What do I want with a puppy?'

Ben was cross at the waste of time such misunderstandings caused. At another house a huge alsatian nearly attacked him and Ben decided that if Dan had come here he'd have been instantly devoured anyway.

By the end of the first street Mrs Thomas called for a break while she drank some squash. Ben hopped around while she sat on a wall, frustrated at the waste of time. They *had* to get on. Then he felt guilty because he couldn't imagine many adults taking so much trouble over a pet. Of course they were really doing it for Peter, but then Ben remembered Mrs Thomas's words about him being just as important. He stopped hopping around and waited patiently.

'Off we go again!' Mrs Thomas said, sweeping her long hair out of her eyes. The second street proved no more fruitful than the first and after the third Ben felt his hopes sinking to zero.

Half way up Conrad Avenue Mrs Thomas noticed a little old lady in her carpet slippers peering anxiously up and down the road.

'Why, that's Miss Hill from church!' Mrs Thomas said. 'I wonder what she's doing standing in the garden?'

Ben frowned. He hoped they weren't going to waste time chatting when there were still five roads to check.

'Is that you, Pam?' Miss Hill called out in a quavery voice as they approached her gate.

'Yes, Miss Hill. What are you doing out of the house?'

'Oh, thank goodness! I thought I was going to have to walk to the phone box. My neighbours are at work, you see. Oh what a terrible thing!'

'What is it?' Mrs Thomas said, taking the old lady's hand.

'I can't turn my gas cooker off, and there's a dreadful smell. It's made me come over quite light-headed.'

Mrs Thomas left Miss Hill at the gate and dashed inside. She returned with a worried look on her face.

'It's not the cooker, Miss Hill, but you're right about the smell. There's a gas leak somewhere in the house. Now, you're not on the phone, are you, so I'll have to run down the road to the phone box and call out the gas people.'

'I'll just sit inside and wait, then.'

'No, that's not a good idea. There could be an explosion or anything. No, you must stay outside or, better still, don't you have a sister in the next road?'

'Ah yes, but she'll be at her flower club this morning. Still, I can go there – it's not too far, just the Legion Hall.'

'Well, Ben will walk with you and wait for me, all right?'

'Oh, what a good lad. I'll just get my stick.'

'I'll fetch that, Miss Hill.'

Ben stood scowling down at his shoes. He couldn't believe this was happening to him. Dan was somewhere out there, waiting to be found and he was wasting precious moments walking an old biddie to the flower club! If only he'd gone with Mr Thomas this would never have happened. Why couldn't she phone up the gas people herself?

'I'm ever so sorry about being a nuisance. Were you going anywhere special?' Miss Hill said, as if she'd just read his thoughts.

'It's all right,' Ben replied as politely as he could manage. There was no point trying to explain. He felt an overwhelming urge to leave Miss Hill and do a runner but he thought better of it. He'd caused enough trouble without adding to it.

'I won't be long now,' Mrs Thomas said, as she fumbled in her pocket for coins. 'I'll get to the Legion Hall as soon as the gas people arrive. Promise me you'll stay there, Ben!'

Ben nodded, a sour expression on his face.

'Don't worry, we'll have time to carry on the search when I've sorted this out,' she added, before jogging away.

'What trouble's that?' Miss Hill said, hooking her bony arm through Ben's.

'I lost our new dog,' Ben said, 'and we were out looking for him.'

'Oh deary me,' Miss Hill sympathised.

Ben tried not to walk too fast but it was agonising to make such slow progress.

'What sort of dog was it?' she asked.

'A black collie cross, called Dan.'

'Hm, black you say?'

Ben's heart leapt. Was she going to say she'd seen him?

'My brother had a black dog once. Mind you, he was called Digger.'

Ben tried to sound interested but he could have screamed. Well, so much for praying. He'd always known it didn't work and this proved it. There wasn't even a chance of finding the puppy now. The gas people would be hours arriving and at this rate they'd reach the Legion Hall by next Wednesday.

'Well, we'd better keep an eye out for this puppy of yours,' Miss Hill continued, 'although my eyesight's not what it was. I expect you're thinking what a nuisance dragging up here with me.'

Ben was silent, wondering whether or not Miss Hill could read his mind.

'If you have faith though, it'll all be all right in the end, that's what I always say. If God means you to find Dan, you'll find him.'

Ben was only slightly encouraged by this. The only chance now was that Peter and his dad were on the trail, but knowing his luck they'd probably encountered flooded roads, fallen trees or had the car stolen by a desperate gang of bank robbers!

Chapter Eight

The door of the Legion Hall seemed the most welcome sight Ben could have imagined. When they got inside, he wasn't so sure. What looked like a hundred ladies were buzzing around the hall like giant bumble bees, stopping to admire vases of flowers which stretched the length of three trestle tables. The air was heavy with the scent of sweet peas and gladioli. Ben was quickly enveloped in a sea of equally floral dresses which brushed his arms and legs as he squeezed through.

'Oh, let me sit down!' Miss Hill sighed, passing her walking stick to Ben. He held it dutifully while she settled herself on one of the chairs behind the table. A cluster of ladies soon gathered round her and there was a great deal of tut-tutting and oohing as she told her gas story over and over again.

'And who knows what would have happened if Pam Thomas and Ben here hadn't come along?' Miss Hill added, beaming up at him.

Ben smiled weakly as attention turned to him. He tried to be patient but it was agony waiting for Mrs Thomas. Where *was* she, and more importantly where was Dan?

'Ladies!' a large voice boomed out from the stage. 'Would you like to take your seats for our coffee break?'

The hubbub died down as people drifted to the sides

of the hall. Ben could see more clearly when they started to sit down.

'I expect we can find some orange squash for you, dear,' Miss Hill said, patting his arm.

Ben sank into a chair with a sigh. It was no good fretting any more. He might as well accept that the morning was over as far as searching for Dan was concerned. Mrs Thomas could be another hour. Ben glowered at the floor, daring anybody to come up and try talking to him.

'I see old Bert still turns up for refreshments!' Miss Hill was saying to her sister Edith.

'Regular as clockwork. Never misses a week. He must smell the coffee,' Edith laughed. 'Course, some of the members object but if you can't give an old fellow like him a cup of coffee it's a poor do, that's what I say.'

'Quite, quite,' Miss Hill murmured in agreement.

Ben glanced up, curiously. He followed Edith's gaze to the far end of the hall. Near the door, well away from the orderly lines of chairs, sat a stooped figure in a tweed overcoat. Ben stared at the grizzled beard and struggled to remember why the old man looked familiar. Suddenly he knew.

'He was in the barn the other day!'

'What's that, dear?' Miss Hill said, bending her head towards him.

'That old tramp – Peter and I saw him near where we live,' Ben explained.

'Really? He doesn't usually move out of Cadmouth centre.'

'Do you know him?'

'Not very well but I see him from time to time and he's a regular here.'

'Why don't they throw him out?' Ben demanded.

'Why should they do that?' Miss Hill asked, surprised.

'He's not in the way and he doesn't cause any bother. I think he enjoys seeing the flowers to tell the truth.'

'He just comes to get a free drink!' Ben scoffed.

'Ah well, it's not much to ask. He's a bit of a local celebrity and we ought to help each other if we can.'

Ben watched disapprovingly as the old man drank his coffee. It didn't seem right to him.

Bert shuffled over to the stage, put his cup down carefully, wiped his whiskers on a sleeve and made for the door. As he passed them, his bright eyes met Ben's and for a moment there was a spark of recognition but he made no sign.

'Morning, Bert!' Miss Hill said cheerfully.

The old man touched his cap respectfully and shuffled by but then he stopped as if he'd just thought of something.

'Got a few coppers to spare, Missus?' he asked, putting his hand out.

Ben made a snorting sound. It was typical – on the scrounge, as usual.

'What for, Bert?' Miss Hill asked.

'Another mouth to feed.'

'Found a friend?' Edith piped up. 'How nice! Give you someone to talk to.'

'Ain't that sort of friend,' Bert muttered.

'Oh, another stray cat!'

'A dog,' Bert corrected. 'Found it last night.'

Ben spun round in his chair clutching Miss Hill's coat sleeve as he did so. She was already tense with excitement.

'Why, Bert, this young boy has lost a puppy! In fact he was out looking for it when I had this nasty gas smell in my house . . .'

Oh no, Ben thought. Not the gas story again.

'What sort of dog is it?' Ben interrupted her. He was

almost afraid of the answer in case Bert said it was a brown spaniel or something.

'It's black.'

'About this big?' Ben asked, holding his hand off the floor.

Bert looked at him suspiciously.

'Could be,' he said.

'Well, I never!' Miss Hill exclaimed.

'Where is he now?' Ben asked.

'I'll have to show you,' Bert said. 'Come on.'

'But I can't, I've got to wait here!' Ben wailed.

'Edith! You stay here and tell Pam Thomas we'll be back directly. Get my stick, Ben.'

Ben could have hugged the old lady. What a sport she'd turned out to be. The odd trio made their way out of the Legion Hall at a stately pace, Bert leading the way. Ben's heart was pounding against his ribs with a mixture of fear, in case it wasn't Dan, and delight in case it was. Oh God, please let it be Dan, he found himself whispering, over and over. He was also thinking that if it *was* Dan, he'd never be mean to another tramp in his whole life. In fact he'd never be mean to anyone in the world again . . . if only Dan could be safe.

Miss Hill wheezed along beside him. Even *she* had managed to quicken her pace a little, in view of the importance of their mission.

'What a day I'm having!' she said, but it looked as if she was quite pleased about it.

They were heading for the car park behind Tesco's supermarket. Ben couldn't imagine where the tramp was going but not long afterwards he turned round to make sure they were keeping up. Next to a rubbish skip there were piles of clean cardboard boxes and Bert bent over one with BAKED BEANS printed on the side.

'Where are you, young fellow?' Bert cooed, as he

rummaged inside it. Ben peered over his shoulder and could have whooped with joy. Dan was curled up on an old jumper at the bottom of the box. As the daylight shone in his eyes, Dan started yelping hungrily but he looked none the worse for his ordeal.

'I 'aven't got a lead for him and he's a slippery little blighter,' Bert grunted, closing the lid of the box before the lithe body could wriggle out.

'Well?' said Miss Hill.

'It's Dan!' Ben breathed, as he squatted beside the box.

'Ah well, I shan't be needing to worry about 'im no more then. You'd best take 'im, young 'un – and be a bit more careful next time.'

Ben stared up at the tramp's lined face with joy shining out of his eyes.

'He'll never get lost again,' Ben promised. 'Thanks for looking after him,' he added. It sounded so useless just to say thanks, when Ben felt as if the tramp deserved a medal at least.

'Come on, I'll carry the box back to the Legion for you,' Bert said, hoisting it up. There was a frantic scrabbling inside as Dan lost his footing. Ben trotted along beside Bert, keeping one hand on the box until he remembered Miss Hill and dragged himself back to her.

'Thank you as well, Miss Hill. I'd never have found Dan if it hadn't been for meeting you.'

Miss Hill smiled. 'I'm just delighted it's all turned out so well. It's even worth nearly getting blown up by gas, I suppose! But didn't I tell you Dan was sure to be found?'

'Yes, you did,' Ben agreed. He also remembered his special prayer that morning. It all fitted into place now. He'd been so angry because of Miss Hill taking them off the search but really she'd been the clue to finding

Dan.

I'm sorry for doubting you, God, Ben said to himself. It would be so easy now to shrug and say it was just a coincidence. Dan would have been found anyway. But Ben knew better. He was sure all their prayers had been answered. He'd learnt some other things too, like not getting fed up waiting, and not thinking everyone else was a waste of time. Miss Hill certainly hadn't been a waste of time. The funny thing was, if the ladies like Miss Hill and Edith hadn't been kind to old Bert, he wouldn't have been at the Legion Hall anyway. And Bert couldn't be so bad if he was prepared to look after lost puppies. He wished he could make up for all the rotten names he'd called the old man.

When they reached the Legion Hall, not only had Mrs Thomas arrived, but so had Peter and his dad. Edith had been telling everyone about Bert's puppy and as he bundled through the door with the cardboard box cradled in his arms a great cheer went up. Peter rushed forward but he didn't need to ask if it really was Dan. Ben's eyes told him the answer.

Mr Thomas took the box, somehow a saucer of milk arrived and Dan was soon crouched in the middle of the floor sending drops of milk over everyone's feet as he lapped at it madly. Peter and Ben squatted beside him, silent with happiness.

Bert was a public hero and he sat drinking coffee and scoffing digestive biscuits with a huge smile on his face.

'Oo,' one of the flower ladies said, sniffing loudly, 'Let me take that box outside, it's getting a bit high in here.'

'Hang on!' Bert protested, retrieving the jumper Dan had used as a bed. 'This was my good one from the last jumble.'

As he held it up the boys noticed two massive holes

in the back. Evidently Dan had used it to chew, as well as sleep on. It was also very smelly. Even Bert seemed to think so, because he sighed and dropped it back in the box.

'I'll be off now!' he said, slipping the last biscuit in his pocket.

'Thanks for looking after Dan,' Peter said politely, offering his hand.

'Yes, thanks a million,' Ben added.

The old man put his hand up to his cap and shuffled off.

'Now,' Mr Thomas said, 'how are the gas people doing?'

'Oh, they're working on it now,' his wife explained, 'and I left them to it.'

'How did you know I was here?' Ben asked.

'Mum flagged us down on the corner of Union Street after she'd phoned the gas company. I wanted to carry on with the search but Dad said we had to come here. I'm glad we did.'

'I know how you felt!' Ben said.

It was a bit of a squash in the car with Edith and Miss Hill but they managed. Dan went berserk, leaping over everyone's laps and licking hands and faces.

'He's glad to be back in the family!' Peter laughed.

At Miss Hill's house the gas workers were busy digging up her path but they gave the all-clear to use the back door.

'Will you be all right now or shall I stay?' Mrs Thomas asked.

'Goodness no,' Miss Hill said, 'I wouldn't dream of it. Edith and I can have a cup of tea and now it's all safe inside there's no need to worry about us.'

'Well, if you're sure.'

'Of course, and please give this to the boys,' she

added, taking a pound coin out of her purse. 'I expect they'd like some sweets.'

'That's very kind. Boys, come and say thank you.'

Peter took the coin with a smile but Ben whispered something in his ear. When he understood, Peter nodded.

'Miss Hill, thanks ever so much for the money but do you think we could give it back to you?'

'But why?'

'So that you can give it to Bert next time you see him. Maybe he'd like to go to the next jumble sale for a new jumper, as Dan ate the last one.'

'It would be our way of saying thanks properly,' Ben added shyly.

'Well, what a lovely idea. Yes, of course. I'll make sure he gets it,' Miss Hill promised.

They waved and then scrambled back in the car where Dan was going mad trying to reach Mr Thomas in the front seat.

'That dog's completely uncontrollable!' Mr Thomas grumbled.

'He'll have to be trained,' his wife agreed.

'That's all right. They run obedience classes at the Legion Hall. We've seen them queuing outside haven't we, Mum?' Peter reminded her.

'Well, I don't have time and I can imagine Dan needing the whole course,' Mrs Thomas said.

'That's OK. We'll do it, won't we!' Ben said, nudging Peter.

'Sure. When shall we start?'

'First class is on the second of September,' Mr Thomas said, 'along with all the night classes.'

'That's the day before school starts,' Peter said. He looked at Ben with a question on his face. 'And . . .'

'No problem,' Ben grinned.

'You're going to stay?' Peter said, slapping him on the shoulder.

'If you like,' Ben said modestly.

Mrs Thomas smiled at her husband.

'Of course we do, Ben. You're one of the family.'

Ben sat back contentedly with Dan's soft body in his arms. He'd found a real home at last, a place where people loved you for yourself and forgave you when things went wrong. And now Ben was beginning to realise there was a bigger family which included Edith, Miss Hill, Bert, in fact everyone who tried to help each other and knew God loved them. He had a feeling that soon he would be part of that family as well.